RED DOG

Louis de Bernières

RED DOG

ILLUSTRATED
BY
Alan Baker

Secker & Warburg
LONDON

Published by Secker & Warburg 2001

1 3 5 7 9 8 6 4 2

Copyright © Louis de Bernières 2001
Illustrations copyright © Alan Baker 2001

First published in Great Britain in 2001 by Secker & Warburg,
Random House, 20 Vauxhall Bridge Road, London SW1V 2SA

The Random House Group Limited Reg. No. 954009
www.randomhouse.co.uk

A CIP catalogue record for this book is available from
the British Library

ISBN 0-436-25617-7   ISBN 0-436-20580-7 (Limited Edition)

Papers used by Random House Group Limited are natural,
recyclable products made from wood grown in sustainable forests;
the manufacturing processes conform to the environmental
regulations of the country of origin

Set in 11 on 13pt Bembo
Printed and bound in Hong Kong by
C & C Offset Printing Co., Ltd

CONTENTS

AUTHOR'S NOTE

The real Red Dog was born in 1971, and died on November 20th, 1979. The stories I have told here are all based upon what really happened to him, but I have invented all of the characters, partly because I know very little about the real people in Red Dog's life, and partly because I would not want to offend any of them by misrepresenting them. The only character who is 'real' is John.

There are two factual accounts of Red Dog's life. One is by Nancy Gillespie, first published in 1983, and now out of print. There is a copy in Perth public library, Western Australia. The other is by Beverley Duckett, 1993, obtainable at the time of writing from the tourist office in Karratha, Western Australia, and in local libraries. Dampier and Karratha public libraries also keep press-cuttings about Red Dog, and I wish to thank their librarians for their invaluable and freely given help.

Non-Australians will find a glossary of Aussie terms at the back of the book.

PART ONE

From Tally Ho to Red Dog

THE STINKER

'Strewth,' exclaimed Jack Collins, 'that dog's a real stinker! I don't know how he puts up with himself. If I dropped bombs like that, I'd walk around with my head in a paper bag, just to protect myself.'

'Everyone likes their own smells,' said Mrs Collins. Jack raised his eyebrows and smirked at her, so she added, 'Or so they say.'

'Well, it's too much for me, Maureen. He's going to have to go out in the yard.'

'It's his diet,' said Maureen, 'eating what he eats, it's going to make smells. And he gulps it down so fast, he must be swallowing air.'

'Tally would let off even if you fed him on roses,' said her husband, shaking his head, half in wonder. 'Shame it's a talent you can't be paid for. We'd all be millionaires.

You know what I think? We should hire him out to the airforce. You could drop him in enemy territory, he'd neutralise it for three days, more or less, and then you could send in the paratroops. It'd be a new era in airborne warfare.'

'Don't light any matches, he's done it again,' said Maureen, holding her nose with her left hand, and waving her right hand back and forth across her face. 'Tally, you're a bad dog.'

Tally Ho looked up at her with one yellow eye, keeping the other one closed for the sake of economy, and thumped his tail on the floor a couple of times. He had noted the affectionate tone of her voice, and took her words for praise. He was lying on his side, a little bit bloated after gnawing on one of his oldest bones. He was only a year old, so his oldest bone was not too old, but it certainly had plenty of flavours, and all the wind-creating properties of which Tally Ho was particularly fond.

Tally was the most notorious canine dustbin in the whole neighbourhood, and people delighted in presenting him with unlikely objects and encouraging him to eat them. With apparent relish he ate paper bags, sticks, dead rats, butterflies, feathers, apple peel, eggshells, used tissues and socks. On top of that, Tally ate the same food as the rest of the family, and at this moment carried in his stomach a goodly load of yesterday's mashed potato, gravy and steak and kidney pie.

This is not to say that Tally ever raided dustbins or browsed on garbage. That would have been very much beneath his dignity, and in any case, he had never found it necessary. He had never lacked success in obtaining perfectly good food from human beings, and ate odd things in good faith, just because human beings offered them to him. He made up his own mind as to what was worth eating again, and whilst he would probably be quite happy to eat more eggshells, as long as they still had some traces of egg in them, he probably wouldn't try another feather.

'I'm going to take him to the airport,' said Jack, 'he can work off some energy, and get some of that gas out.' He went to the door and turned. Tally Ho was looking up at him expectantly, both yellow eyes open this time. His ears had pricked up at the magic word 'airport'.

'Run time,' said Jack, and Tally sprang to his feet in an instant, bouncing up and down with pleasure as if the floor was a trampoline. The caravan shook and the glasses and cutlery in the cupboard started to rattle. Tally Ho seemed to be grinning with pleasure. He was shaking his head from side to side and yelping.

'Get him out before he demolishes the whole place,' said Maureen, and Jack stood aside for Tally Ho to shoot out of the door like the cork from a bottle of champagne. He bounded out of the small garden, and did some more bouncing up and down outside the car. Jack opened the back door, said 'Hop in' and Tally Ho jumped onto the back seat. In an instant he hopped over and sat in the front seat. Jack opened the front passenger door and ordered 'Out!'

5

Tally looked at him coolly, and then deliberately looked away. He had suddenly gone deaf, it appeared, and had found something in the far distance that was terribly interesting.

'Tally, out!' repeated Jack, and Tally pretended to be looking at a magpie that was flying over the caravan.

Jack used to be in the Australian army, and he liked his orders to be obeyed. He didn't take it lightly when he was ignored by a subordinate. He picked Tally bodily off the seat, and deposited him in the back. 'Stay!' he said, wagging his forefinger at the dog, who looked up at him innocently as if he would never consider doing the slightest thing amiss. Jack closed the door and went round to the driver's side. He got in, opened all the windows, started the engine and called over his shoulder, 'No bomb-dropping in the car. Understood?'

Tally waited until the Land Rover had started off down the road, before springing lightly once more over onto the front passenger seat. He sat down quickly and stuck his head out of the window, into the breeze, so that he would have a good excuse for not hearing his master telling him to get in the back. Jack raised his eyebrows, shook his head and sighed. Tally Ho was an obstinate dog, without a doubt, and didn't consider himself to be anyone's subordinate, not even Jack's. It never occurred to him that he was anything less than equal, and in that respect you might say that he was rather like a cat, although he probably wouldn't have liked the comparison.

6

Seven kilometres away the car stopped outside the perimeter fence of Paraburdoo airport, and Tally Ho was let out. A Cessna light aircraft bounced along the runway and took off. Tally chased its shadow along the ground, and pounced on it. The shadow sped on, and Tally ran after it in delight, repeatedly pouncing, and wondering at its escape.

Jack got back into the car, and drove away. He blew the horn, and Tally pricked up his ears.

It was a red-hot day in February, which in Australia is the middle of the summer, and all the vegetation was looking as if it had been dried in an oven. It was one of those days when you are physically shocked by the heat if you go outdoors, and the sun feels like the flat of a hot knife laid directly onto your face. The air shimmers, distorting your views of the distance, and you can't believe that it really is that hot, even if you have lived there for years, and ought to be used to it. If you have a bald patch, and you aren't wearing a hat, it feels as though the skin on the top of your head is made of paper and has just been set alight. It seems as if the heat is going straight through your shirt, so you go as fast as you can from one bit of shade to another, and everything looks white, as if the sun has abolished the whole notion of colour.

Even the red earth looked less red. Visitors to that place can't believe that the mining companies are actually allowed to leave all those heaps of red stones and red earth all over the place, without caring about it at all, but the strange fact is that all those heaps and piles were put there by nature, as if She had whimsically decided to mimic the most untidy and careless behaviour of mankind itself. The difference is that nature managed to do it all without the help of bulldozers, diggers and dumper trucks. Through this ungentle landscape galloped Tally Ho, raising his own little plume of red dust in the wake of the greater plume raised by Jack Collins' car. His whole body thrilled with the pleasure of running, even though the day was at white heat, and even though he had to blink his eyes against the dust. He was young and strong, he had more energy than his muscles could make use of, and the world was still fresh and wonderful. He understood the joy of going full tilt to achieve the impossible, and therefore he ran after his owner's car as if he could catch it with no trouble at all. As far as he was concerned, he really did catch it, because after seven kilometres there it was, parked outside the caravan, its engine ticking as it cooled down, having given up the chase, too tired to continue. As for Tally, he could have run another seven kilometres, and then another again, and caught the car three times over. When he arrived home he came leaping through the door, headed straight for his bowl of water, and slurped it empty. Then, his tongue hanging out and leaving drips along the lino, he went back outside and lay down in the shade of a black mulga tree.

That evening Mrs Collins opened up a big can of Trusty, and Jack set his stopwatch to zero. Tally Ho had a special gift for bolting food at lightning speed, and so far his record for a whole 700g can was eleven seconds flat. Tally Ho put his forepaws up on the table to watch the meat going into his bowl, and Mrs Collins put on her curt tone of voice and said, 'Down, Tally! Lie down!' He slumped down on the floor, and put on his most pathetic and appealing expression, so that she felt sorry for him even though she knew it was only an act. He sighed, and raised first one eyebrow and then another. His whole body was quivering with anticipation, the muscles in his legs just waiting for the moment when he could hurl himself at his dinner.

'Are you ready?' asked Mrs Collins, and Jack Collins nodded. She put the bowl down on the floor, Tally leaped up and Jack pressed the timer on his stopwatch. 'Crikey,' he declared. 'One hungry mongrel! Ten point one seconds. Truly impressive.'

Tally cleaned his bowl conscientiously with his tongue, and then cleaned it again just to make sure. When there was definitely not one atom of food left in it, he strolled outside and lay down once more under the shade of the tree, his stomach feeling pleasantly stretched, and very soon he fell asleep. He dreamed of food and adventuring. When he awoke half an hour later, fully restored, he lay for a while, enjoying the way that the evening was cooling off, and thought about going walkabout. He felt curious about what might be going on in the wide world, and the thought of missing out on something made him feel uneasy. He got to

9

his feet, stood still for a time whilst he thought a little more, and then set off past the other caravans, and into the wilderness. He found a path worn through the spinifex by kangaroos, and set off joyfully down it, quickly losing all sense of time, completely absorbed by all the mysterious smells and noises. He was sure that he could find a bilby or a quoll.

In the morning Jack Collins said, 'I think Tally's gone bush again,' and Maureen Collins replied, 'I'm worried that one day he's going to disappear for ever.'

'Don't say that,' said her husband. 'He always comes back eventually.'

'It's the call of the wild versus the call of the supper-dish,' laughed Mrs Collins.

'He always seems to come back well fed, though.'

'Maybe he's got other people who feed him.'

'Wouldn't surprise me,' said Jack. 'Tally's no slouch when it comes to tucker.'

Three days later, just when the couple had almost given up hope of ever seeing him again, Tally Ho reappeared, bang on time for supper. He was dusty, his stomach was nice and full, his nose had a long scratch on it courtesy of a feral cat that he met on the roo-trail, and he was grinning with self-satisfaction. That night he polished off a big can of Pal in nine seconds flat.

RED DOG GOES TO DAMPIER

The time came when Maureen and Jack Collins had to move from Paraburdoo to Dampier, a long hot journey of about 350 kilometres, along a difficult, rutty dirt-track. In some places there are water-courses that cross the road, so that your vehicle can get buried up to the axles in mud, and you get completely stuck there until another vehicle arrives to pull you out. People usually take a couple of days' worth of food and water with them, just in case.

The road runs alongside the railway line that takes the iron ore from Mt Tom Price to Dampier, and often you see trains so long that you cannot possibly count the number of wagons, heaped up with red earth, that need three vast locomotives to pull them slowly through that immense wilderness.

Before leaving Paraburdoo for that long trek, Jack Collins took the precaution of opening all the car windows so that the breeze would blow through and stop it turning into an oven, and began to pack it with the more precious and breakable things. Bigger and heavier items he packed into the trailer that they had hitched to the towbar on the back.

In the kitchen of the caravan, Maureen Collins packed an esky with cold drinks and sandwiches, because there weren't too many decent places to stop for refreshment, and for the same reason she remembered to put some dunny paper into the front glove box of the car. You never knew when you might have to stop and take a short stroll into the crinkled cassia.

When they were ready to go, Jack called Tally Ho and opened the back door of the Land Rover. 'Up, dog!' he commanded, and as Tally jumped in Jack quickly shut the door and jumped into the driver's seat before the dog could leap over and occupy it. Tally

12

looked disgruntled, and thought about clambering over into Maureen's lap. It was against his principles to share a seat with anyone, however, so he sighed and reconciled himself to settling down in the back with his chin resting on a box.

It was early in the morning when they set off, because it was much cooler then. There would be less chance of the car boiling over, and anyway, it was pleasant to travel when the day was fresh and new.

They had hardly gone fifteen kilometres, however, before Tally's stomach began to get to work on his breakfast, and a foul stink rolled over the two unfortunate folk in the front. 'Oh, my God,' exclaimed Maureen, 'open the windows! Tally's done it again!'

'They're already open,' said her husband, pinching his nose with one hand and controlling the steering-wheel with the other as they lurched over the ruts and corrugations of the road.

Maureen rummaged in her bag and found her

13

bottle of scent. She poured a little onto her handkerchief, and held it to her nose. Jack thought that dogstink and lavender made a strange mixture.

Tally let off another one, even worse than before, and Maureen turned round and told him off. 'Bad dog!' she scolded, 'stop it at once, d'you hear?', but Tally just looked offended and puzzled, as if to say, 'What's she going on about?'

They had not gone much further before Jack had to stop the car, even though they were in the middle of nowhere. He got out and opened the back door. 'Out!' he commanded, and Tally leaped down to the ground, thinking that he was about to get a nice walk in the gum-trees. His heart was beating a little bit harder at the thought of all those shovel-nosed snakes and emus.

Jack grabbed Tally under the armpits and lifted him into the trailer, amongst all the furniture and the boxes of bits and pieces, saying, 'Sorry, mate, but if you can't hold it in, you're not coming with us. You're lucky we're not leaving you and your horrible reeks out here in the desert.' He tapped Tally on the nose with one forefinger, saying, 'Good boy! Stay!'

Tally looked up at him reproachfully, hoping that if he looked sad it might persuade his master to let him back into the car, but to no avail. As the car set off once more, he settled down between the legs of a chair and watched the world go by. There was nothing he loved quite so much as travelling from one place to another, simply for the pleasure of seeing what was going on.

'Do you think he'll be all right?' asked Maureen, looking behind her. 'The wheels are throwing up an awful lot of filth.'

Jack glanced in the rearview mirror, saw the great cloud of dust that they were trailing behind them and said, 'Well, I'd rather have Tally get dirty than have to put up with all those stinks.'

Four hours later they arrived in Dampier. Both had done their share of the driving, because it was hard work to keep the wheel steady on such a bad road, and both she and her husband had aching shoulders and stiff limbs.

They clambered out of the car, stretched, fanned their faces with their hands because of the heat, and went to see how their dog was. When they saw him they put their hands to their mouths and laughed. Tally looked up at them and wagged his tail disconsolately. All they could recognise of him were two sorry-looking amber-yellow eyes, because the rest of him was an inch thick in dark-red dirt and dust.

TALLY HO AT THE BARBECUE

'Why don't you take Tally for a scamper on the beach?' asked Maureen. The evening had brought pleasantly cool temperatures, and in any case she fancied the idea of having the house to herself for a while.

Jack looked at his watch. 'Might be a nice idea,' he said, 'I've got some time to kill before I go on shift, and Tally could do with a run. Couldn't you, mate?' Tally seemed to agree, even though he had just been missing for several days, and had only recently returned, and so the pair of them set off for Dampier beach, just when the western sky was beginning to turn gold at the edges. A collared kingfisher sang 'pukee, pukee, pukee' as it flew overhead, and a posse of fork-tailed swifts sang 'dzee, dzee, dzee' as they swooped in the opposite direction, rolling and darting after insects. Man and dog made their way down to the beach, where a gentle swell was dropping wavelets onto the sand. Opposite was the strangely named East Intercourse Island, and south-west of that you could see Mistaken Island huddling in the sea, though no-one seemed to know who had originally been mistaken about what, in order for it to have earned itself such a quirky name. The beautiful islands of the Dampier Archipelago lay strung out across the ocean.

A man was fishing off the beach with a handline, hoping to catch a garfish for the pan, but what really interested Tally Ho was the delicious, rich, juicy smell of frying steak, lambchops and sausages. His ears pricked up, his mouth watered and every nook of his brain began to engage itself in mischievous plans. Jack Collins sensed what was going on, and took hold of Tally's collar before he could run off.

As they walked down amid the barbecues, Jack was puzzled and amazed by the number of people who seemed to know Tally Ho already. 'Look, there's Red Dog!' said one man, and another patted him on the head and said, 'Hello, Bluey, howya goin'? Welcome to the barbie.' Jack Collins realised that Tally must have made a lot of acquaintances in his times off. It occurred to him that perhaps Tally had already attended a few barbecues on this very beach, which was a popular place for the local folk to come and cook up in the evenings.

He relaxed his grip for just one moment, and Tally

17

took that chance to leap free and scamper away. Jack called after him, but Tally was too busy to hear and too obstinate to obey. What Jack saw next made the blood rise to his cheeks from sheer embarrassment.

There was a man lifting sausages off his grill with a fork and bending down to put them on a plate that was on a rug beside him. On the plate were some salad and some new potatoes. When there were three sausages on the plate he straightened up to collect a burger from the grill, and when he looked down again, he had to look twice. There were no sausages. He gasped with surprise and shook his head in puzzlement. He scratched his head and looked around. Everyone was minding their own business. 'Me snaggers!' he said, 'someone's swiped me snaggers!' He called to the man next to him, ''Ere, mate, did you swipe me snaggers? 'Cause if so, I want 'em.'

The man turned his head briefly, 'Not me, mate. I got me own. If you want one, you're welcome.'

'I'll be damned,' said the first man, 'they were just there and then there they were, gone.'

Jack Collins called after Tally, but the dog was licking his lips to get off the last lovely traces of sausage-grease, and planning his next foray. He went down on his stomach and laid his head flat on the sand, with his nose pointing in the direction of a nice succulent steak that had just been put on a plate. The man who was about to eat it looked away for a second, and Tally darted in and snatched it, leaving his victim with nothing but a sliced tomato and a few scrapings of mustard. Tally bolted the steak and set off in search of a burger that he could smell quite distinctly at the other end of the beach.

'Did you swipe my steak?' the second man accused his neighbour, and 'Who swiped me snaggers?' called the first man, soon to be joined by 'Bloody 'ell, where the devil's me burger?'

Jack saw all this and crept away as quietly and inconspicuously as he could. He knew that Tally would find his own way home, and he wasn't going to hang about to be blamed for his dog's behaviour. An angry miner wasn't the kind of man you'd want to have a blue with.

RED DOG MEETS JOHN

'I don't think he's coming back,' said Maureen Collins.

'It's easily the longest he's ever been away,' said Jack, shaking his head. They felt a little sad, as though they had both known that they were going to lose him, and had been trying not to think about it.

'I hope he hasn't been run over.'

'We would've heard. In a small place like this, all the news goes round in a flash. Anyway, that one's got more lives than a cat.'

'I heard,' said Maureen, 'that he's been going from door to door, bludging.'

'He's got a knack for locating tucker, that's for sure,' said Jack.

'I suppose he's probably all right, then. Still, it's a shame. I miss the little fella.' Tally had finally left home.

20

Unlike most dogs, who are happy to spend the day either sleeping or watching life go by, he found life too interesting to stay in one place. He wanted to see what the world was like, wanted to know what was going on round the next corner, wanted to join in with things.

He was too bright to spend his time being bored, and, whilst there were a lot of people he liked, he hadn't yet found anyone he could really love, the way that dogs are always supposed to love. There wasn't anyone to be devoted to. He would call in on Jack and Maureen from time to time, and he would always be happy to see them. He might stay a couple of days, and get fed and watered, but he and they knew that he had moved out for ever.

It was lucky for him that the town was so full of lonely men. There had been a few aborigines and even fewer white people there before the iron companies and the salt company had moved in, but just recently a massive and rapid development had begun to take place. New docks were constructed, new roads, new houses for the workers, a new railway and a new airport. In order to build all this, hundreds of men had arrived from all corners of the world, bringing nothing with them but their physical strength, their optimism and their memories of distant homes. Some of them were escaping from bad lives, some had no idea how they wanted their lives to be, and others had grand plans about how they could work their way from rags to riches.

They were either rootless or uprooted. They were from Poland, New Zealand, Italy, Ireland, Greece, England, Yugoslavia, and from other parts of Australia too. Most had brought no wives or family with them, and for the time being they lived in big huts that had been towed on trailers all the way up from Perth. Some of them were rough and some gentle, some were honest and some not. There were those who got rowdy and drunk, and picked fights, there were those who were quiet and sad, and there were those who told jokes and could be happy anywhere at all. With no women to keep an eye on them, they easily turned into eccentrics. A man might shave his head and grow an immense beard. He might go to Perth for a week, go 'blotto on Rotto', and come back with a terrible hangover and lots of painful tattoos. He might wear odd socks and have his trousers full of holes. He might not wash for a week, or he might read books all night so that he was red-eyed and weary in the morning when it was time to go to work. They were all pioneers, and had learned to live hard and simple lives in this landscape that was almost a desert.

These brawny individuals took a rapid shine to Tally. They had little affection in their lives, and they could feel lonely even with all their workmates around them, so it was good to have a dog that you could stroke, and have playfights with. It was good to have a dog to talk to, who never swore at you and was always glad to see you. Tally liked them, too, because they ruffled his ears

22

and roughed him up a bit, and rolled him on his back to tickle his stomach. They fed him meaty morsels from their sandwiches and dinner plates, and they brought him special treats from the butcher. Even though he was sometimes absent for days on end, there would always be a can of dogfood on the shelf, along with all the tools and oily rags, and there would always be a bit of steak left over from the weekend's barbecue.

No-one knew his real name, and before long he was simply called 'Red Dog'. A dog is happy to have lots of names, and it was no bother to him if someone wanted to call him 'Red'. In any case, a red dog is exactly what Tally was. He was a Red Cloud kelpie, a fine old Australian breed of sheepdog, very clever and energetic, but some people thought that Red Dog might have had some cattle dog in his ancestry. He was one of three puppies, and Tally turned out a lovely dark, coppery colour, with amber-yellow eyes and pricked-up ears. His tail was slightly bushy, and on his shoulders and chest the fur was thick like a mane. His forehead was broad and his nose was brown, a little bit turned up at the end. His body was solid and strong, and if you picked him up you were surprised by how heavy he was.

Red Dog and the men from the Hamersley Iron Transport section got to know each other, because one of their bus drivers adopted him and became the only person to whom he ever belonged.

John was not a big fierce man like some of the

23

miners. He was small and quite young, and he loved animals almost more than anything else. He had high cheekbones because he was half Maori, and people used to say of him that he was a friend to everyone. One day John met Red Dog in a street in Dampier, when he was standing outside his bus waiting for some of his daily passengers to arrive. When he caught sight of Red Dog he reacted with instinctive pleasure, crouching down on one knee and saying, 'Hey, boy! Here!' and clicking his fingers and tongue. Red Dog, who had been busy with his own thoughts, stopped and looked at him. 'Come on, mate,' said John, and Red Dog wagged his tail. 'Come and say g'day,' said John.

Red Dog came over and John reached down and took his right paw. He shook it and said, 'Pleased to meet you, mate.' John took Red Dog's head in both hands, and looked into his eyes. 'Hey, you're a beauty,' he said, and Red Dog knew straight away that from now on his life was going to take a new direction.

When the miners turned up to take their big yellow bus to work they found John sitting in the driver's seat, and Red Dog sitting in the seat behind him.

RED DOG AND NANCY GREY

One day someone turned up on the bus whom no-one had ever seen before. Nancy Grey was new in town, having come to work as a secretary at Hamersley Iron, and she had never heard about Red Dog.

When she got on the bus to go for her first morning at work, she found it full of miners, and with no empty seats, except for a seat behind the driver, which had a red dog in it. She looked at the rows of men grinning at her, and she gazed at the red dog, who looked away as if he had not noticed her.

None of the men offered her their seat, because they wanted to see what would happen when Nancy tried to move Red Dog.

'Down!' said Nancy, who wasn't going to take any

nonsense from an animal. Red Dog looked up at her, and settled himself into his seat more firmly.

'Bad dog!' exclaimed Nancy, and Red Dog curled his lip and gave a low growl. Nancy was a little bit shocked, and drew back but at the same time she was almost sure that this dog would never bite her. His expression wasn't quite fierce enough. The men in the bus began to laugh at her. 'You'll never get him out of there!' said one.

'That's his seat,' said another. 'No-one sits there when Red wants it.'

Nancy faced the men, and began to blush. It was embarrassing to be outfaced by a dog and a busload of miners. Determined not to give in, she sat down gingerly on the very edge of the seat, where Red Dog wouldn't be disturbed.

Red Dog was disturbed, however. This was his seat, and everyone knew it. What was more, the whole seat was his, and not just a half of it. Ever since he had met John, he had travelled around as much as he wanted on the company buses, no matter who the driver was, and he always had the seat behind the driver. It was emphatically his seat, and no-one else's. He showed Nancy his teeth and growled again.

'Well, aren't you a charmer?' she said, but she didn't budge.

Red Dog could see that threats weren't doing any good, so he decided to push her off the seat. He turned around, stuck his muzzle under her thigh, and pushed.

She was surprised by how strong he was, and she was almost tipped off. Behind her the men began to laugh again, and she grew even more determined.

'I'm not moving,' she told the dog quietly, 'so you'll just have to put up with me.'

Red Dog wasn't going to give in either, and he pushed Nancy until she only had one tiny bit of her backside on the seat. He felt that he had made his point, and let her perch there, uncomfortable as she was.

The next day Nancy got on the bus again, and there was Red Dog, sitting behind the driver's seat once more. 'Oh, no,' she thought, because once again the bus was full, and all the men were waiting to see what was going to happen. The people in the office had told her about the dog after she had got into work the previous morning, and now she knew that this was the dog who travelled around as the fancy took him. He lived mostly in the transport workshops, keeping an eye on

27

what was going on, and he was a paid-up member of the Transport Workers' Union. When the action in the workshop got too slow, he got lifts all over the area. Sometimes he travelled on the water-truck, sometimes in the company utes, sometimes in the giant train-trucks.

As he got to know more and more people, he began to take lifts in their private cars as well. You had to watch out for Red Dog when you were driving, because he never forgot a vehicle that he had had a lift in, remembering both the paintwork and the sound of the engine, and he would wait by the side of the road until one of them came along. Quite suddenly he would run out in front of the car so that you had to screech to a halt and let him in, so you learned to watch out for him in the same way that you watched out for rock-wallabies and wallaroos. Red Dog always insisted on the front seat, especially on the company buses, even more especially when John was driving, and that was that.

Nancy sat down a little closer to Red Dog than she had yesterday, and he looked sideways at her, showing the whites of his eyes, as if he were about to bite her. Instead he got down, stuck his muzzle under her thigh and once more tried to push her off. Nancy was conscious of the sniggers of the men in the bus, and, mustering as much dignity as she could, she said, 'None of you's a gentleman, that's for sure.'

Red Dog seemed a little put out by this remark and

he sat up and pretended that there was no-one else on his seat. If he couldn't move that obstinate woman, he would just have to treat her with the disdain that she deserved. He let her put a little bit more of her backside on the seat.

The next morning Red Dog realised that he was looking forward to sitting next to Nancy, and when she sat next to him he forgot to try to push her off. He thought that he might just try being a bit aloof, but when she said 'Hi, Red!' and patted him on the head, he couldn't help smiling a little in the way that dogs do. He thumped his tail on the seat, once only, and then went back to looking out of the window, not wanting to give way too much to begin with.

Nancy didn't turn round, but she could tell that the miners were impressed, and weren't mocking her any more. She knew that she had scored a victory over them at the same time as she had won over Red Dog.

From that moment onward, Red Dog and Nancy became friends. There were not many others who dared to try it, but Nancy sat next to him whenever she liked.

NANCY, RED DOG AND JOHN

There weren't many single women around the place in those days, so if one of them turned up, it caused a lot of excitement and interest in all the single young men. They speculated as to what she would be like and whether anyone had a chance of going out with her. If anyone was spotted chatting up a girl, the other men would rib him about it, saying, 'Fancy your chances, eh, mate?' and 'What makes you think she'd go for a skinny little runt like you, when there's proper blokes like us?'

John got to know Nancy a little because Red Dog let her sit next to him behind the driver's seat of the bus, so that he was able to have snatches of conversation with her as he was driving along. They first got to talk properly because one day Red Dog made a smell so bad that they had to evacuate the bus completely, until it was safe to go back on. Even Red Dog got out and waited, wagging his tail and being friendly, as if he expected to be congratulated.

John looked shyly at Nancy, and she smiled back. They both bent down to pat Red Dog on the head, and their hands touched. They both laughed, a little embarrassed, and John said, 'Did you hear what happened yesterday? There was a new driver on the bus, and he tried to throw Red out.'

'Really?' said Nancy.

'Yeah, and Red Dog wasn't having it, and he was growling at this driver, and then the blokes started shouting and jeering at him.'

'And then what?'

'Well, the blokes made it clear what was what, and the new driver had to let Red stay on. Anyway, when the driver asked about it at the depot, we told him all about Red, and now he knows better.'

'I saw something funny the other day, a bit like that,' said Nancy. 'Red was in the shopping mall, and you know it says "No Dogs" on the door, and he was lying there in the entrance because it was like an oven out-side, and he likes the air-conditioning, and no-one ever tries to move him because he isn't just any old dog.'

'Yeah, I know,' said John.

'Well, there's a new woman working in the mall, right? She's called Patsy or something, and she didn't know about Red. She sees him lying there, and all the

blokes have come in because it's lunchtime, and they're sitting around eating their sandwiches and legs of chicken. Anyway, Patsy sees Red Dog and orders him out, and he refuses to move. So she grabs him by the collar and drags him out, with his feet sliding on the tiles because he's determined not to go. She closes the door, and before you know it Red Dog's come back and he's lying down exactly where he was before. Patsy starts to kick up a fuss, and tries to drag him out again, and then all the fellas start having a go at her, you know, cat calling and throwing chicken bones and orange peel, so finally she gives up, and now she knows not to bother him again.'

'That's my dog,' said John, and one of the miners tapped him on the shoulder. 'Listen, mate. We've got to get to work, so be a good fella and see if it's safe to get back in.' John put his head in the bus and sniffed. Then

he announced 'Sorry, guys, it's still a bit ripe. You'll have to wait a bit more.'

The miners groaned, and John said to Nancy, 'There's a new film on at the Open Air. Would you like to come and see it?'

'What is it? she asked.

'Can't remember,' said John. 'Supposed to be good, though.'

'All right then,' said Nancy. 'I'll take your word for it.'

On the evening of their date John cleaned out his car and sprayed it with air freshener and mosquito repellent. He shaved carefully so that he didn't cut himself, splattered his face with slightly too much aftershave, and put on a clean new shirt and freshly pressed trousers. He had had a haircut that afternoon, and had polished his shoes. The only things left to do were to give Red Dog the slip, and pick up Nancy. Picking up Nancy

33

wouldn't be difficult, but Red Dog would certainly give him a problem, because Red was so devoted to him that he followed him nearly all the time, and couldn't bear to let him out of his sight for very long. When John played football, Red Dog ran onto the pitch and joined in, and when John was playing cricket, Red Dog would find out about it somehow, run onto the pitch, get to the ball before the fielders, and then play keep-away with it.

John was determined not to let Red Dog interfere with his night out with Nancy, so he called Red Dog and told him to hop into the car. He drove him all the way to the Hamersley Iron Transport section and left him there, telling the drivers to keep him busy at all costs. Then he went to pick up Nancy, and drove her all the way to Karratha to the Open Air cinema.

He parked the car alongside all the other ones, and very soon the lights went down and the film began. John had unrolled the sunroof, and the stars sparkled in the sky above them. It was a lovely warm evening, and the crickets were scraping away in the long grass. John held out a can of Emu to Nancy, saying, 'Like a stubbie? It's good and cold.'

'No, thanks, John,' said Nancy, shaking her head. 'Never could get a taste for beer.'

John was disappointed because he liked to have a beer himself, but he knew that it wasn't very nice to kiss someone who has been drinking it, when you haven't had any yourself. It tastes horrible and stale. As he was hoping to kiss Nancy later on, he reluctantly decided not to have one himself. He pretended to be watching the film, whilst thinking about how to put his arm round Nancy's shoulder without it being too obvious. He waited for a scary bit in the film, and when Nancy squealed, that was when he put his arm around her, just to comfort her, of course.

The next problem was working out how to kiss her, and there just didn't seem to be a decent opportunity. He thought he would probably have to wait for that awkward moment when he was leaving her at her door and wishing her goodnight.

She laid her head on his shoulder and snuggled up a little, so that John was able to put a small kiss on her temple. Things were definitely looking up. He was about to take the risk of kissing her properly, when there was an urgent scratching on the door of the car. John had several scratches on it by now, where the paint had been scraped away.

'Oh no,' he said.

'What was that?' asked Nancy.

'It's Red,' said John. 'He's found us.'

Red Dog scratched again, and John sighed.

'Aren't you going to let him in?' asked Nancy.

'Not if I can help it. You know what he's like.'

'Don't be mean, John. Let him in.'

'He comes to see all the films,' said John, 'and he always wants to sit with someone he knows. He must've got a lift.'

'I'll let him in,' said Nancy. She opened the back door, and Red Dog jumped in, his tongue lolling happily and his tail wagging.

'You shouldn't've done that, Nance,' said John.

For a while it looked as though everything was going to be fine. Red Dog settled down in the back and watched the film, becoming excited only when there was an animal on the screen, and John managed to get his arm around Nancy during another scary bit. Once more her head rested lightly on his shoulder, and once more John kissed her lightly on the temple. Red Dog put his feet up on the back of the seats before him, and pushed his head in between them. 'He's jealous!' laughed Nancy, and John told him to get back down and be quiet. A romantic scene was developing in the film, and John chose his moment to move in for that big kiss on Nancy's lips, when a horrible stink rolled over them from the back of the car.

'Strewth,' exclaimed John, and Nancy opened the door and jumped out. 'Red,' said John, wearily, 'you're a real dag of a dog.'

Red Dog looked pleased with himself, and John and Nancy never did get to have that kiss. It was one more romance that nearly happened. John used to say that as long as Red Dog was his companion, he probably wouldn't be allowed to have a girlfriend.

RED DOG
AND THE POSH POOCHES

One day Red Dog was lying under the workbench at Hamersley Iron Transport section, when he began to grow restless. There was not much going on, and he didn't really feel like travelling around on the buses today. He had befriended one of the drivers of the enormous locomotives that took the iron ore from Mt. Tom Price to Dampier and had been all the way on it, back and forth several times. It took a very long while, but it was good to sit in the driver's cabin and watch the landscape go by. In the evenings he saw wallabies and kangaroos, and he liked the look of the pools shaded by white gum trees in the places where creeks ran through.

Today, though, Red Dog did not feel like spending several hours on a train, even if he could visit Paraburdoo afterwards by getting a lift with one of the miners. Today Red Dog had a feeling that something interesting was going on. He had an excellent instinct for knowing when something was about to happen, even turning up to supervise operations when some-body was moving into a new house, and then attending the house-warming party a couple of days later.

Red Dog got onto one of the long yellow buses that was going into Dampier. There was somebody in his seat, so he growled until the man said, 'OK, OK, Red, I get the message' and ungrudgingly gave up his seat and moved to the back. At the junction with the main road Red Dog tugged at the sleeve of the driver, and kicked up a fuss until he stopped. He alighted there and went to wait for a car that he recognised.

Shortly he detected the noise of Patsy's engine. It had loose tappets and a small hole in the exhaust. As soon as it appeared he ran out in front of it, and Patsy skidded to a halt.

'You nearly gave me a heart attack,' she said as she reached over to the passenger door to let him in. Red Dog leaped in and made strange motions with his head, which Patsy rightly interpreted as a request to open the window on his side. They drove off together, he with his head out of the window to catch the breeze, and she recovering her equanimity after such a sudden halt. 'One day,' she said to Red Dog, 'you're going to get munched by a car.'

Red Dog made no kind of acknowledgement. He was used to being told off, and accepted it with the same amused indifference that an elephant would display if complained to by a mouse. Patsy accepted that Red Dog had his own ideas, too. She had learned the hard way, because she had been the one who had tried to throw him out of the air-conditioned supermarket. Since then she had grown to like and respect him as much as everyone else, and always watched out for him in case he needed a lift. She had once taken him to the vet as well, but that's another story.

They drove past the glistening white salt beds of the Dampier Salt Company, and past the narrow gully of Seven Mile Creek. It seemed to Red Dog that he could smell just a hint of lots of other dogs on the wind.

Patsy wanted to turn right to go to the industrial estate at Karratha, but Red Dog had other ideas. He made her stop at the turning, and jumped out through the window, crossing the road and then trotting off into the town centre. He amused himself for a while by chasing the shadows of birds, and pouncing on them, and then he caught that smell of dogs again.

Red Dog liked some other dogs, but he often got into fights with the ones that he didn't. He was never afraid of a fight, but was annoyed by being dabbed with stinging antiseptics, so he avoided fights unless it was absolutely a matter of personal honour or extreme dislike. In this case he didn't catch a whiff of any of his enemies. He followed his nose until he arrived at a patch of wasteland that would one day be a carpark for

Karratha City shopping centre, and found to his delight that there was indeed something interesting going on.

Most people had cattle dogs or kelpies, or mongrels, but some people in the Pilbara had pedigree dogs. These folk were proud of their animals, and regretted never having a chance to show them off, so they had formed a kennel club, and begun to organise shows and competitions. They met up on agreed dates, judges were appointed, rosettes and certificates were made in advance, and competitors obsessively snipped off stray hairs, shampooed and combed coats, tried to disguise blemishes, and put their pets through strict regimes of obedience training.

Here they all were. There were whippets from Whim Creek, Rottweilers from Roebourne, poodles from Port Hedland, cairns from Carnarvon, Pekinese from Paraburdoo, pugs from Pannawonica, corgis from Coral Bay, Dalmatians from Dampier, English sheepdogs from Exmouth and even a mutt from Mungaroona, which its owner was claiming to be a new breed.

They had got to the point in the proceedings when all the competitors were lined up in a row, waiting to step forward for their awards, and when all the judges were conferring in order to add up points and finalise their decisions.

Red Dog surveyed this curious scene with much interest and decided that, of all the people there, the judges were clearly the most important. In order to make his mark he walked with great dignity up to their table, and peed onto one of its legs. Having thus left his visiting card he paraded slowly along the line of smart dogs and their equally smart owners. The dogs he ignored altogether, but he recognised many bitches that he had flirted with all over the Pilbara, and whom he visited whenever he could get a lift in their direction. He greeted them happily with sniffing and playfighting, much to the horror of their owners, whose comical and panicky attempts to shoo him away he ignored.

The judges in the meantime were watching Red Dog's intervention with both concern and amusement. Some of them had given Red Dog lifts in their own cars, and knew that he was a local celebrity. In later years they would even vote to have a picture of his head as the official badge of their club, but just now they were wondering what to do. Red Dog saved them any further trouble, however, because, having paraded along the line in one direction, he now paraded along it in the other, as if he himself were a judge with some difficult decisions to make.

Finally he went over to the judges' desk and peed on it again, although this time on a different leg, and then he decided to go home. He loped off back to the roadside, and waited for a familiar car. This time it was Nancy Grey who took him back to Dampier, and she made extra sure that all the windows were wide open.

One of John's friends telephoned him that evening and told him what his dog had been up to that afternoon. John looked down at Red Dog, who was fast asleep in the corner, and laughed. He said, 'I'm surprised that he didn't just jump right up on that table and award himself all of the prizes.'

RED DOG'S EXPENSIVE INJURY

One morning Nancy, her fingers shaking with anxiety, telephoned the transport section of Hamersley Iron. She rang when the men were having smoko, and got through almost straight away. 'Is John there?' she asked. 'It's really important.'

John came to the phone, and as he listened to Nancy, his face turned pale. 'It's about Red,' said Nancy.

'Why what's happened? What's up?'

'Look, John, I'm sorry to have to tell you this, but Red's been shot.'

'Shot? What d'you mean, shot?'

'I found him, just now. He was dragging himself along the road, near Seven Mile Creek. Someone's shot him.'

43

What John said next, about whoever it was that had shot his dog, can be left to the imagination. He swore and cursed, and then, realising that Nancy was still on the phone, he said, 'Sorry about that, Nance, I couldn't help it.'

'It's all right, John,' she said, 'I've been feeling the same way. You've got to be sick in the head to go round shooting dogs.'

'Where is he?' asked John.

'Well, I had Patsy in the car and she's stayed with him at Seven Mile Creek while I came in to find a phonebox. Look, I'm nearly out of coins. I'll get back there and wait for you, OK?'

John put down the phone and, white-faced, worried and angry, turned to the blokes who had been listening to his side of the conversation, with their cups of tea halfway to their lips. 'Where's the nearest vet?' he asked.

'Port Hedland,' said Jocko, who was originally from Scotland, but had been in the Pilbara for several years.

'Strewth, that's four hours' drive,' exclaimed John. 'He could bleed to death before we get there.'

'I'll come with you, mate,' said Jocko, 'I'll do the first aid.' He was a part-timer with the St John's Ambulance Brigade, and there wasn't much he didn't know about staunching blood.

'I'm coming too,' said Giovanni, who was known to everyone as 'Vanno'.

'And me,' said Piotr, who was known as 'Peeto'.

John went to see their supervisor, and came back a

few minutes later. 'The good news is that we can go, and he's going to organise a whip-round to pay for the vet. He's calling up some of the blokes so we've got enough drivers on the buses. The bad news is that we get the day's pay docked.'

The men's faces fell somewhat, but not one of them changed his mind about coming along. Red Dog was special, and this was a genuine emergency. He had ridden around in the buses with each one of them, they were fond of him and proud of him, and it was worth losing a day's pay for Red Dog's sake.

Jocko 'borrowed' one of the First Aid boxes from the workshop, and they ran outside and piled into John's Holden. Off they went at high speed, raising a cloud of russet dust behind them until they reached the tarmac of the public highway.

At Seven Mile Creek they spotted Nancy's car, with Patsy and Nancy kneeling beside it at the roadside, tending to the sad bundle of red fur that lay in the stones. They piled out of the car, and John reached down and ran his hand over Red Dog's head, 'Hello, mate,' he said. Red Dog wagged his tail feebly at the sound of his master's voice. 'What've they done to you?' asked John. Red Dog laid his head on the ground as if he were too tired to think of anything any more. He felt a terrible stinging and aching in his leg, and his thoughts had become hazy and disconnected. It was like being in someone else's dream, a dream where you can't understand what is going on, because it isn't yours.

45

'Jeez, look at that,' said Peeto. He gestured towards the dog's haunch. The rusty coat was matted with dark-red blood, and fresh scarlet blood flowed from somewhere beneath the fur. John could hardly speak. He thought that Red Dog was bound to bleed to death, and this made him so sad that his throat felt as though it would never loosen up again. He didn't want to shed tears in front of his mates, and they knew how he was feeling because they felt the same. This dog had become a fair part of their lives, and they felt that dread in the pit of their stomachs that comes when you know that you are about to lose someone you love.

'What d'you think, Jocko?' asked John.

Jocko got down on his knees in the dust and opened the First Aid box. He got out a small pair of scissors and began to clip away the fur from around the wounds. Carefully he removed the clippings, and soon he had exposed two small dark holes from which blood was steadily streaming with each beat of the dog's heart. He cleaned the wounds with antiseptic, and took a closer look. 'We've got to stop this so that the blood gets a chance to clot,' he said, almost to himself, and he made two small plugs out of cotton wool, soaked them in surgical spirit, and put them gently into the holes. Red Dog twitched from the pain, but made no fuss. Jocko made two big pads out of gauze and taped them over the area of the wounds. He stood up and looked at the others. 'Should do the job,' he said.

46

Nancy said, 'Is it OK if we leave you boys to it now? Can you manage all right?'

'Should be fine,' said John. 'Listen, you two have been really tops. I can't thank you enough, I really can't.'

'Anything for the old devil,' said Patsy, and she bent down and ruffled Red Dog's ears. 'You'll be right,' she said.

The two women drove away, waving their hands out of the windows, and John tossed the car-keys to Peeto. 'You drive, mate, I'm going in the back with Red.' He lifted the dog in his arms and Jocko opened the car door for him. He got in with some difficulty, and Jocko got in the other side. Red Dog lay across them, his head in John's lap, with Jocko beside him, ready to deal with any emergency that might occur.

Peeto drove a bit faster than he should have. For the most part they said little, but every now and then one of them would voice his anger against whoever it was who had shot Red Dog.

'I'd like to put him through the ore-crusher at the mine,' said Vanno. 'Yes, I would.'

'I'd like to get a chance to munch him,' said Peeto. 'I'd like to be at the zebra crossing just when he gets there, and I'd stop for him nice and polite, and then I'd put my foot down and knock him flat.'

'I'd just like the chance to punch him in the face,' said Jocko. 'Just once. For the satisfaction. Then I'd walk away.'

John was just looking down at Red Dog, breathing heavily in his arms, and he said, 'Don't die, daggy dog, don't die.' He kept looking at the wounded leg, as if looking might make it better.

Peeto drove right up to the limit, and soon they were speeding along the North Coastal Highway. They passed through Roebourne, once such an important town, now so abject and neglected, over the dry beds of the creeks, and on towards Sherlock Homestead. The men couldn't help noticing how many kangaroos and wallabies had been hit by cars, and lay dead in horrible attitudes at the side of the tarmac.

'They should do something about it,' said Vanno. 'I just counted ten in five k's.'

'They should put up fences,' said Peeto.

'They jump fences,' said Jocko. 'And anyway the farmers want them run over, right enough, so who's going to put them up?'

'I'm just wondering,' said Vanno, 'why there's any of them left when there's so many on the highway.'

'It's because there are so many,' said Jocko. 'There's an endless supply.'

'Anyway,' said Vanno, 'they're so stupid, they see a car with lights on and they hop in front, and bang, that's that. One big mess and no more roo. You know, once I saw a wallaby at the side of the road, OK? It was early, very early, and I slowed down for him and I let him hop across, and just when I put my foot down to get away, he hopped back straight out in front, and there's nothing I can do. Not one thing. What can you do with a critter as dim as that?'

48

Jocko stroked Red Dog's back and said, 'You better watch out, old boy, 'cause the way you jump out, one day you're going to be like all these roos.'

The sun poured scalding light onto the flat grassland, creating strange mirages of islands floating in water above the horizon. There were mirages on the road ahead too, so that sometimes Peeto didn't know whether or not it was safe to overtake the tractors and heavy-laden lorries. The journey seemed to take for ever, and John suffered the continual torment of wondering if Red Dog would live long enough to get to the vet at all. He seemed very quiet and still and his breathing had become light and irregular. His owner was still feeling an awful fear in his stomach that made him feel sick, and he was thinking about all the fun that he and the dog had ever had together, and might never have again. When they did finally arrive in Port Hedland after nearly four hours' driving across that harsh landscape, he felt as if he had already been to the moon and back.

Peeto drove the car straight to the old part of town, by the waterside, and stopped outside a newsagent's shop in Wedge Street. Vanno jumped out, and ran in. 'Where's the vet?' he asked bluntly, and the woman reached under the counter for a Yellow Pages. She handed it over to him, Peeto leafed through it hurriedly, memorised the address by reciting it to himself a couple of times, and ran back out to the car. 'Well, thank you too,' called the woman after him in a very sarcastic tone of voice.

They were fortunate that they happened to arrive in Port Hedland during surgery hours, and that the vet wasn't too busy with other clients. When John walked in with Red Dog in his arms the vet was just dealing with his last client of the day, a cat that had come in for her regular check-up.

'What have we here?' said the vet, looking at the four worried men in the uniforms of Hamersley drivers, with battered akubras on their heads. 'Bring him in, boys.'

The vet asked John to lay the dog on the table, and he lifted the dressing that was now dark with dried blood. 'Nice job,' said the vet. 'Who did this for you?'

'It was me, mate,' said Jocko. 'Hope it was up to scratch.'

'Couldn't have done better,' said the vet. 'You're in the wrong job.'

'Glad I didn't stuff it up.' Jocko looked proud of himself, and Vanno clapped him on the back. 'Good on ya,' he said.

'Will he be all right?' asked John.

50

'Too early to say,' said the vet. 'First thing is I'll have to get those bullets out.' The vet looked at the animal a little more closely and exclaimed, 'Well, I do believe it's Red Dog.'

'Jeez,' said Peeto, 'how did you know that?'

'This dog,' said the vet, 'everyone knows. The first time I met him, it was at Pretty Pool, and we were waiting to watch the stairway to the moon, and we'd all brought stuff for the barbie, and Red Dog here, he ate my salami, and he got my neighbour's steak. Everyone knows Red Dog.'

'He's been here a lot?' asked John, astonished. Red Dog followed him about faithfully for most of the time, and it was hard to imagine when he might have found the opportunity to travel so much.

'Every time anything's going to happen,' said the vet, laughing, 'along comes Red Dog in a road-train, and then when it's over off he goes. It's my belief he's got a couple of girlfriends hereabouts, 'cause just recently I've noticed some of my youngest clients look just a little bit like him.'

'Good lad,' said Jocko, stroking his muzzle.

The men sat outside in the waiting room whilst the vet and his nurse extracted the bullets. They couldn't think of very much to say to each other, and just kept exchanging glances, and wiping their brows with the backs of their hands. The suspense was too much to bear, as it seemed to them that Red Dog was fighting for his life and could very easily lose the battle.

After half an hour or so the vet came out and told them, 'I think he'll be fine. Lucky for him, the bullets missed the bone. He probably lost a lot of blood, but he's strong and obstinate, that's for sure. Give him a while to wake up, and we'll see how it goes.' He held out his hand and dropped the two distorted bullets into John's outstretched hand.

John looked down at them and shook his head. 'What I don't understand,' he said, 'is why anyone wants to go around shooting at dogs.'

'You'll be surprised,' said the vet. 'It happens all the time, and I take out more bullets than I'd ever expect. It's the farmers and the station men. They'll shoot anything that looks like a fox or a dingo or a dog, and they say they're protecting the stock, but if you ask me half of them are trigger-happy morons who do it for the sake of it. They're the kind of people who still eat damper and think they're starring in a western. I've heard of people driving around with hunting rifles sticking out of the windows, blasting away at anything that moves. It makes you despair, it really does. The only thing that's worse is when they go round leaving poison bait. That's what really gets me riled. It makes you sick to see a dog die of strychnine. If they could see how horrible it is for a dog to die of poison, I don't believe they could bring themselves to do it.'

Before long the men were called into the surgery, and found Red Dog, his wound heavily dressed, lying motionless but awake on the table. 'I doubt he'll be able to move,' said the vet, 'but he'll certainly recognise you.'

The four fellows made a fuss of him, and Red Dog sighed happily. 'I've got to keep him a couple more hours,' the vet told them, 'so why don't you go out and get a bite, and come back later? I don't mind hanging about. I've got paper to shuffle about in the office.'

John looked at his watch, and said, 'Well, I reckon it is tucker time.'

Jocko pulled a face; 'I've just realised I haven't told me missus where I'm gone.'

'You're for it,' said Vanno. 'I bet you a dollar she's cooking something up right now.'

'I'll give her a tinkle,' said Jocko.

The men turned to leave, and Red Dog, thinking he was going to be left, struggled to his feet and made to jump down. 'Hey, you,' said the vet, 'you're not going anywhere.' He told John to keep the dog still, and gave him another dose of sedative with the hypodermic. 'I can honestly say,' said the vet, 'that I've never known a dog as ill as this do anything like that before.'

They made their way to the Bungalow Café and ordered plenty of food. They ate with the appetite of men who have been reprieved, and it put them into a thoroughly good mood. 'What say we find a bar?' said John. 'It's my shout. Least I can do.'

They started off with a couple of middies each, and then Peeto said he'd taken a yen for a Bundy, 'just to top it off.' The others declared it a fine idea, and they had a

53

Bundy each. 'Here's to Red Dog,' said Vanno. 'Chin chin.'

'Long life and good health,' said Peeto.

'Lots of girlfriends and lots of pups,' said Jocko.

'Here's to you lads for helping me out,' said John.

They knocked back their Bundies, and sighed with satisfaction. 'Just one more,' suggested Peeto.

'Let's have a Scotch,' said Jocko, licking his lips and raising his eyebrows. 'It's a special occasion, is it not, and nothing's better than Scotch.'

An hour later they staggered out of the pub, happy and hazy, full of beer and Bundie, and made their way back to the vet's. There they found Red Dog in spirits almost as good as their own, and such was their state of happiness that they read the sum at the bottom of the vet's bill several times before they appreciated how big it was. 'Would you mind,' asked John, 'if we paid you later? Some of the boys are having a whip round.'

'We haven't got this much,' said Peeto.

'If we pay it now we couldn't buy enough petrol at the servo to get us home,' said Vanno. 'We'd have to push it all the way from Whim Creek.'

The vet looked at their anxious and slightly drunken faces, and decided he could take the risk of deferring payment, but he warned, 'I don't think any of you should be driving. You've had a few too many.'

Such was their confidence, inspired by alcohol and relief, that the four fellows decided to drive home anyway. Somewhere near the Sherlock River bridge, however, they realised that behind them was a car approaching quickly, with its blue light flashing.

'Oh, jeez,' said Peeto, 'it's the coppers.'

'We'll help you pay the fine,' jested Vanno, and then regretted it later.

Peeto pulled in to the side, and got out of the car as the policeman approached him with his notebook at the ready. 'Hello, Bill,' said Peeto.

'I'm not Bill when I'm on duty, mate,' said the policeman, who was in fact one of Peeto's neighbours.

Peeto couldn't resist saying, 'And when you're on duty I'm not "mate". I'm "sir".'

That was Peeto's big mistake. No-one with any sense should be cheeky and clever with a traffic policeman who has been on duty for six hours and has become so bored with sitting at the side of the road in his car that he is in just the right frame of mind for being nasty to someone.

Peeto failed the breathalyser test, and the policeman wouldn't let him off, even though he had been one of the saviours of the famous Red Dog.

Next day during smoko they worked out how much it had all cost. There was the loss of the day's wages, the cost of the petrol, the food and the booze, there was the vet's bill, and the fine for driving whilst under the influence of alcohol.

'Hey,' said Vanno glumly, 'what say the next time we fly a surgeon in? It's gotta be cheaper than this.'

RED DOG
AND THE WOMAN FROM PERTH

One evening John was sitting in his hut drinking tea, when there was a scratch at the door. It was Red Dog's scratch, so he got up to let him in. Just as he was reaching the doorhandle, however, there was also a knock. 'Strewth,' thought John, 'Red's learned a new trick.'

He opened it, and there was Red Dog with someone he had never seen before. She was a woman in early middle-age, with a tightly permed hairstyle and a worried but resolute expression.

'Sorry to bother you,' she said, 'but I've come about the dog.'

'I'm not selling him,' said John. 'In fact I'd sooner sell me mum. If she was still alive, that is.'

'Oh, I don't want to buy him,' said the woman. 'I've

just come because I'm worried about him, and I know he's yours.'

'Belongs to everyone, really,' said John, 'but I'm his best mate. What's up then?'

'It's the ticks,' said the woman.

'Ticks?'

'Yes. Look, my name's Ellen Richards, and I just moved up here from Perth, and I've got a job at Hamersley, in the admin office, and I heard there's a problem with ticks round here.'

'Yes,' said John, 'you burn 'em on the backside with a hot needle, and they drop off, and you kill 'em in metho.'

'Yes,' said Ellen. 'It's just that Red Dog visited me this evening, and I couldn't help noticing that he's got ticks.'

'He gets them sometimes,' said John. 'I check him every couple of days.'

'Well, I checked him too,' said the woman, 'and I found some on his ears and one on his back and I burned them off, but there are some strange browny pink ones on his stomach, and I can't get them off; and when I try to burn them off, he just squeals. I'm worried about it, and as he's your dog, I thought I ought to let you know.'

It was John's turn to be concerned. 'Ticks on his stomach?'

'Yes, on both sides.'

John called Red Dog and rolled him over on his back. He lay there with his paws in the air, wondering

57

whether his master was going to rough him up and tickle him, which was very acceptable, or whether the woman would be coming at him with hot needles again, which definitely was not. 'Where are these ticks?' asked John.

The woman knelt down and pointed. 'Look,' she said, 'there's about four or five on each side.'

John was horrified. 'You haven't been putting hot needles on those?'

'Yes,' she replied, 'but they wouldn't drop off.'

John scratched his head in disbelief. 'And he squealed, did he?'

'Oh yes. It was horrible. I think that when I burn them they just bite into him harder. Maybe you should take him to the vet.'

'Listen, lady,' said John, 'I can't think of a nice way to put this, but those aren't ticks.' He paused, thinking how best to express himself. 'You've never had a dog of your own then?'

'Oh, yes, I've had several.'

'Were they dogs or bitches, then?'

'Both. I've had both.'

'And you've never noticed?'

'Never noticed what?'

'They've all got . . . well . . . they've all got tits. Even the dogs. They don't use 'em, but they got 'em.'

Ellen put her hand to her mouth. 'You mean?'

John nodded, 'Those aren't ticks, they're tits.'

She went pale and sat down on John's only chair;

58

'Oh my God,' she said, 'and I've been putting hot needles on 'em.' She forgot about John and went down on her knees. She put her arms around Red Dog's neck and started to cry 'Oh, Red, I'm so sorry I hurt you. I'm so sorry, so sorry . . .'

Red Dog looked up at John, sharing this moment of embarrassment. Red liked to be hugged as much as the next dog, but not necessarily by somebody who was whining and wauling in his left ear, and whom he didn't know very well at all.

The next day, much to her shame, and much to the amusement of the workers at Hamersley Iron, Ellen discovered that the news of her mistake had got to work even before she did. 'Watch out for your tits, mates,' called the men, covering their chests with their hands, and pretending to run away.

It took years for Ellen to live it all down, but Red Dog came and visited her anyway, because he could forgive anyone who was generous with food, and she'd soon given up all that painful business with hot needles and methylated spirit.

HAS ANYONE SEEN JOHN?

John bought a nice powerful motorbike because, although he already had a car, he liked the idea of riding around on hot days with the breeze blowing in his face. It was great for short journeys, as long as you weren't carrying much with you, and anyway, the girls quite liked a man with a motorbike as long as he wasn't a crazy driver. Once or twice he put Red Dog on the seat in front of him, with his paws on the petrol tank, but he didn't seem to like it very much, greatly preferring the comfortable seats of trucks, buses and cars. When John kickstarted his bike, Red didn't make any moves to come too, as he always did when his master started up the car. Instead he lay in front of the door, waiting for John to come back, or he consulted his encyclopaedic memory, and took a stroll to one of the houses where somebody might have fed him years before. Sometimes in the fierce summer he went to the shopping centre where Patsy had once tried to kick him out, and lay in the air-conditioned cool of one of the shops, seeming to know by instinct when John was due to return.

One night John went to have a meal at the house of a couple of friends, and he took the bike even though it was July and the nights had been very cold indeed. Red Dog was out on patrol, looking for other dogs to fight with and cats to chase, and by the time he came back, John had already gone to dinner.

What happened after that dinner will always be a mystery.

John had some beers, but he wasn't too drunk to drive. He was in a happy mood, because of the company of his friends and the good meal they had given him, and there didn't seem anything wrong with the bike as he started it up and drove off down the road. His friends waved him goodbye and went back inside to clear up and go to bed.

There is a sharp bend on the road coming into Dampier, and the turning is very abrupt in the place where John had to turn off. In the undergrowth around the verges are heaps of the great red rocks that make the landscape of the Pilbara so particular.

John never made it round the bend of the road. Perhaps he misjudged his speed, perhaps there was a stone in the road that made him skid, or perhaps the beer had affected his judgement more than he realised. Perhaps the cable on his accelerator jammed. It is just as likely that a wallaby suddenly hopped out in front of him, and he tried to swerve to avoid it.

Whatever it was, John lost control of the motorbike, hit the kerb and went flying through the air. As bad luck and destiny would have it, he landed on a rock, which caved in his chest.

No-one knows how long John lay dying on that freezing night, with no-one except Red Dog to realise that he was missing. John did try to crawl back to the roadside, and perhaps if he had reached it he might have been found in time. However, he was too weak and too greatly hurt. After a while that gentle animal-loving man, who was a friend to everyone, died all alone in a rocky patch of spinifex. Perhaps he dreamed about Red Dog as he faded away into that long last sleep, on such a cold and starry night.

The next moming John did not appear for work and Peeto and Jocko and Vanno wondered what had happened to him.

'I got a bad feeling,' said Vanno, shaking his head.

'It's not like John,' said Peeto. 'He phones in if he's not coming.'

'Let's give him 'til smoko, and if he's still not here by then I'll go out and look for him,' said Jocko.

John was not there by breaktime, and so Jocko went round to John's hut. He found Red Dog waiting out-side the door. The dog got to his feet and greeted

Jocko with some relief. 'Where's your mate?' asked
Jocko, and Red Dog flattened his ears and wagged
his tail. It always gave him pleasure when someone
mentioned his mate.

Jocko knocked again, and waited for a while. If John
was there, he wouldn't have locked his dog out. John's
Holden was parked outside, but there was no motorbike leaning against the wall round the back. With a
sinking feeling in his heart, Jocko remembered that the
previous night John had said that he was going out to
eat with friends. Jocko went back to the depot and rang
them up. 'John left at elevenish,' he was told. 'Why?
What's up?'

'Was he on his bike?'

'Yes.'

'He never got home,' said Jocko.

Jocko borrowed a company ute and drove over
to the friends' house. He had a brief word, and then
drove back in the direction of John's accommodation.
He thought about the time when he used to have
a motorbike himself, and watched the road with the
eye of experience. There were always places that were
especially dangerous for motorcyclists, such as where
there were potholes, or loose gravel, or places where
kangaroos and wallabies crossed at night. When he came
to the sharp bend, he stopped the car and got out. He
wandered over to the other side and looked down into
the hollow.

It was a very small community back then, and everyone knew everyone else. John had been well liked, and for several days everybody felt a sense of shock and loss. People's minds went numb. They didn't want to have to talk. Everyday things seemed too trivial to discuss, and if somebody tried to make a joke, somebody else told him to shut up. John had been so young, much too young to die so suddenly and so senselessly.

Now no-one would know what John might have achieved with his life, whether or not he might have started a business, whether he might have married and had children, or whether he might have gone back to New Zealand to start a new life with his pockets full of Hamersley cash. He had died with the best part of his life still to live, leaving behind him only his grieving friends, who would have fond memories of him for ever, and a devoted pet dog who had no idea what had occurred, and never would.

Amid all the sadness and the arrangements for the funeral, everyone forgot about Red Dog, and it wasn't until three days had passed that anyone noticed that he was still waiting outside John's hut. John's friends brought food, which Red Dog would eat, before lying down in the dust with a heavy sigh to wait once more, even sleeping there through the chilly nights, and waking in the dawn with his russet coat glistening with dew.

After three weeks Red Dog came into the transport depot in case John was there. The drivers treated him as an old friend, and to begin with he spent half his time in the depot, and half his time waiting for John outside his empty hut.

When John failed to appear, Red Dog could only think of one thing. No-one knows how much language a dog has, or exactly how it thinks, but Red Dog's mind was full of a single great question: 'Where is John?'

There is only one thing worse than losing the one you love the most, and that is losing them without knowing why. If you are a dog, then your master is like a god to you, and the pain of losing him is greater still. Red Dog's heart was sick with longing, he had only one desire, and he had only one plan. He went to every place that he and John had ever visited together, and sniffed in every corner to find a trace of his master. When the scents faded he looked up into the face of each person he met, hoping that somehow they might divine his trouble and lead him out of it. If he could have spoken, he would have said over and over again, 'Has anyone seen John?'

It was from this time that Red Dog became the Pilbara Wanderer, the Dog of the North-West, who belonged to everyone because he couldn't find the one he loved the most, and wouldn't settle for less.

PART TWO

The Dog of the North-West

LOOKING FOR JOHN

Red Dog had his greatest adventures after John's death. He had always enjoyed his freedom, but he had always had John to return to. Now he took absolute liberty, and refused to give it up. He would have given it up, no doubt, only if he had been able to find his master. Being such a well-loved and well-known local character meant that almost every week somebody tried to adopt him, to make him comfortable, and to feed him up so that he would settle down and stay. Red Dog liked these people, and if their children were sick he would even wait patiently by the bed until they were better. Then one day they would come out of their house and find Red Dog by the car, waiting to be driven away on his next great quest. With sadness in their hearts, the people who had hoped to own him would drop him off wherever it was that he wanted to go, and it might be months until one evening there would come that imperious scratching at the door, signalling his temporary return. Red Dog simply treated people as people treat their friends, dropping in, and then passing on.

Red Dog travelled as usual on the Hamersley Iron buses, in their utes, and in the train to Mt Tom Price. Keenly he looked at everyone they passed. People noticed that he still seemed to be searching.

Red Dog travelled the 900 kilometres to Broome, a magical tropical town where there are tata lizards that wave to you every few seconds, where there is Cable Beach, whose waters in the summer are as warm as a bath, where the raindrops are as big as plums, where divers bring pearls from the bottom of the sea, and where there are salt-water crocodiles in the mangrove swamps, who like nothing so much as to swallow a nice plump dog.

Red Dog went there with a road train, and stayed for two weeks, eating every night at the local hotel. He looked everywhere, but couldn't find John, and so he came back very slowly in an ancient car crammed to the brim with a large family of aborigines.

One day he happened to be outside her caravan when Patsy was loading up her car for her holiday. It was midsummer, and the tropical heat was unbearable for many of the folk of the Dampier Archipelago. The March flies were stinging anyone who went outdoors, and warnings were being issued about not letting the sun shine directly onto fuel tanks. They had been known to explode, with fatal consequences. Patsy had made friends with Ellen, the unfortunate lady who had made the mistake about Red Dog's ticks, and these two had planned to go to Perth with Nancy Grey, because Perth is 3,000 kilometres to the south and is cooler and breezier. Because Ellen had come from Perth originally, they were planning to stay with her relatives, and anyway, sometimes women like to go off and have fun together, without being inhibited by men.

'Hello, Red,' said Patsy, and he gave her his dog's version of a smile. 'Got nothing to do?' she asked.

'Why don't we take him with us?' suggested Ellen. 'He might enjoy it.'

'Want to come to Perth?' asked Nancy. 'If you're lucky, we might even take you to Freo.' She patted the seat beside her, and the dog jumped into the back. Women smelled nice, and often gave you sweet things to eat, so it struck him as a good idea to go on a trip with them. It was because of women that he had acquired a taste for chocolate.

The three had clean forgotten that Red Dog was not necessarily very good company in a confined space, and they spent the two days' drive making disgusted expressions and exclaiming, 'Pooee! Pooee! Oh, my God, I can't believe it! Not another one!' The dog stuck his head out of the window to enjoy the breeze in his face and to make it easier to keep an eye open for John, so he had no idea of the torture endured by the three

71

women, who would remember this trip for the rest of their lives, and not just because of the smells.

What happened was that they went to Cottesloe beach, a long beautiful stretch of sand, opposite Rottnest Island, where people like to go for walks, to do their exercise, and to take a swim after work. Some people get up early and have breakfast in one of the cafés overlooking the sea. Sometimes friendships spring up because one meets the same folk over and over again, and dog owners get to know each other's pets first, and only after that do they get to know each other.

Patsy, Ellen and Nancy were sunning themselves on the beach after a swim in the surf. Red Dog loved the surf, and devoted much time and energy to trying to round it up, as if he were a sheepdog and the waves were some very strange and difficult variety of sheep. He had also pounced on the shadows of lots of seagulls, and had caused much distress in one small boy by mistaking his model aeroplane for a bird. By the time he had jumped on it and given it a good biting, it was too late to repair the mistake. He had joined in with one game of frisbee, another of volleyball, and another of beach cricket, in which he had briefly confiscated the ball, forcing the cricketers to chase him up the beach.

The three women dried themselves after their swim, and lay down in the sunshine. In those days nobody bothered much about whether or not the sun was bad for your skin, and so they were planning to get as suntanned as possible before they went home, where just now it would be too hot to lie in the sun at all. They frequently compared forearms in order to see who was getting the brownest.

'Let's go to Rotto tomorrow,' suggested Nancy.

'Oh, yes,' exclaimed Patsy. 'I'm dying to see the quokkas. They're supposed to be really sweet.'

'Well, they are,' said Ellen, who had seen them many times before, 'but they're not exactly bright. Sweet and stupid, that's what they are.'

'They don't allow dogs, do they?' said Nancy. 'What'll we do with Red?'

Ellen suddenly sat up; 'Where is he anyway?'

They searched up and down the beach, and they asked everybody they saw, particularly those with dogs. No-one had seen Red Dog at all. They whistled and called, and then they enquired in the local cafés and hotels, in case he was busy befriending the chefs. They went into Fremantle, and they searched Mosman Park.

'You know what we've done?' asked Patsy. 'We've only gone and lost the most famous dog in Western Australia.'

'In all of Australia, probably,' corrected Ellen.

'When we get home, they're going to kill us,' moaned Nancy. 'What are we going to do?'

'Just imagine,' said Ellen, wide-eyed, 'Jocko and Peeto and Vanno, and the other drivers, they'll go crazy.'

The holiday was ruined. They went to see the quokkas, but it wasn't enough to cheer them up. They went to the best fish restaurants at the water's edge, but found that they couldn't eat. They shopped for souvenirs, but didn't find anything that they really liked.

They cut their holiday short and drove home. It took them another two days, taking turns at the driving, and they hardly said a word. They remembered Red Dog, with his head out of the window, and the awful smells he made, and they felt completely miserable.

When at last they reached home, late at night, they found Red Dog waiting for them outside Patsy's caravan. He had hitched a lift home from a truck-driver who recognised him. He hadn't liked Perth all that much, with its bottle-brush and peppermint trees, its pretty yellow sourgrass, its military-looking Norfolk Island pines, and its shiny modern buildings. He preferred the tougher life up north, with its poverty bushes, its Brahminy kites, its silvery river gums, its rock wallabies, its Ruby Saltbush, and its deep red stones. Besides, he had been to Perth before, with John, to that very same beach, but this time there had been no sign of him at all.

The three women fussed over him and fed him, with a sense of relief such as they had seldom experienced before, and after that they told him off for ruining their holiday and causing them so much guilt and worry. Then Nancy pointed out that they had a few days of their holiday left and suggested, 'Why don't we make the most of it, and go to Exmouth?'

74

'Yeah, why not?' agreed the other two. They looked over at Red Dog, and Ellen said, 'Are we taking Red?'

'No chance,' said Nancy.

'Not on your life,' confirmed Patsy.

In the morning they piled back into the car and with light hearts headed south once more on the North West Coastal Highway.

Red Dog called in on the new vet in Roebourne, and then he went to Point Samson and Cossack. He visited Jocko, Peeto and Vanno at Hamersley Iron, and afterwards he went and stayed for a night at the Walkabout Hotel in Karratha, where the chef was one of his providers. Finally, he surprised and astonished the three women by turning up in Exmouth three days later. They spotted him walking by when they were all having a milkshake at a café. He seemed pleased to see them, but by the next morning he had hitched a lift to Onslow.

RED DOG AND RED CAT

Red Dog used to call in quite frequently on the caravan park where Nancy, Patsy, and Ellen were living whilst the new houses were being built. It was a pleasant enough place, with tubs of flowers set out on either side of the pathways, and people's washing hanging on lines.

The only thing wrong with it was that there was a rule that stated NO DOGS, and a caretaker who not only did not like dogs, but was determined to enforce the rule. His name was Mr. Cribbage, and whenever he saw Red Dog he tried to shoo him away. Later on Red Dog was to cause Mr Cribbage a considerable amount of trouble, but right from the start he also caused some trouble for Red Cat.

Red Cat definitely approved of the rule about NO DOGS. In fact, Red Cat hated dogs so much that if he had been dictator of Australia, he would probably have had all the dogs executed. There was no rule forbidding cats in the caravan park, and so Red Cat very much liked it there. Red Cat was the boss of all the cats in Dampier.

He was a ginger tom, big, muscly and mean. He had green eyes and tatty ears, he had a slantways scar on his nose, he had a white bib on his chest, and a tail that was barred in lighter and darker shades. He had great big paws, and when he stretched them out, the claws would spring from their sheaths like curved swords. When he sat on your lap and purred, you could feel the vibration shaking the bones in your head. When you dangled a string in front of him to make him play, you made very sure that your fingers were out of his reach. When he caught a rat, you could hear the crunch of its bones as Red Cat munched it up. When he yowled and wauled at night to attract the lady cats who were the mothers of his kittens, it sounded as though a baby was being tortured to death. When he ate his dinner, he could, if he chose, wolf it almost as fast as Red Dog. Red Cat had never lost a fight.

If Red Cat saw a dog, his policy was to jump on its back, dig his claws in, and ride it around the caravan park until it was too tired and terrified to run any more. Then Red Cat would jump off and swipe it across the nose, leaving four parallel scratches that trickled with blood. Then, when the dog rolled over and surrendered with its paws in the air, Red Cat would parade proudly away, the tip of his tale waving with self-satisfaction. More often than not, the dog would not come back to risk this treatment again.

Red Dog liked chasing cats, and had plenty of rake-marks on his snout to prove it. He was a cleverer dog than most, but like most dogs he had never really managed to learn that a dog always loses a fight with a cat, because eventually the cat will turn round and lash out. Red Dog was an optimist, and he sincerely believed that just because a cat runs away to begin with, then he must already be the winner. Anyway, it was such fun doing the chasing that, as far as he was concerned, it was worth getting scratched for it later.

When Red Dog explored the caravan park for the first time, he walked around the back of Nancy's allotment, and came face to face with Red Cat. Red Dog was overcome with excitement, and leaped forward to give chase.

He stopped a fraction of a second later, however, because Red Cat did not turn and run. He sat quite still, and opened his mouth and hissed. Red Dog was impressed by the pink tongue and the two rows of shiny white teeth.

He pounced again, but still Red Cat did not run. This time he flattened his ears and hissed again, even louder. Red Dog began to have doubts, but he couldn't resist having another try. Red Cat stood up, arched his back, flattened his ears and hissed, even more loudly. Red Dog sat back on his haunches, puzzled by this unusually valiant cat, but something made him have another try. Red Cat bushed up his tail, made the fur stand up on his back, flattened his ears, hissed, and hit out so quickly that Red Dog didn't even know what had happened until his nose began to sting and drip with blood.

Just as Red Cat wasn't going to be frightened by

Red Dog, neither was Red Dog going to be frightened by Red Cat. He bared his teeth and growled. Red Cat bared his teeth and hissed. Red Dog barked in anger. Red Cat spat.

Red Cat tried to spring onto Red Dog's back, so that he could ride him around with his claws well stuck in, but Red Dog dodged out of the way just in time. Snout to snout, growling and hissing, neither animal would give ground. Red Cat scratched Red Dog again. Red Dog tried to bite, but missed. Then Nancy came round the corner and interrupted the whole confrontation.

There was now a new vet in Roebourne, which was much closer than Port Hedland, and the new clinic wasn't even properly completed yet. The young vet looked at the deep slashes in Red Dog's nose, and tutted as he cleaned and stitched them. 'It's funny,' he said, 'but I saw a dog just like this last week. Had a thorn in his paw. Different owner, though. And the week before, somebody else brought in a dog just like this for immunisation. It's weird. Hard to believe there's so many dogs that all look the same.'

Nancy smiled to herself. Red Dog was everybody's dog now, and anyone would take him to the vet if there were need of it. People were taking bets to see how long it would be before the vet realised that all the different Red Dogs that looked the same were in fact the same Red Dog. So far he had been to the clinic five times, and the vet had still not put two and two together.

80

When Red Dog returned to the caravan park he sniffed around until he found the freshest trail that Red Cat had left behind. There was something about that cat that interested him. He eventually tracked it to a patch of silver saltbush, where it was lying in wait for rabbits, and for just a short time they put on a repeat performance of the hissing and growling.

Eventually it all seemed too much bother, however, and people were surprised to see them sitting side by side watching the evening coming down, listening to the kangaroos thumping out in the wilderness, just like two old folk on a bungalow verandah.

They were unlikely friends, but friends is what they certainly became. Red Cat still hated dogs, but for Red Dog he made an exception. When Red Dog turned up at the caravan site, Red Cat would come bounding up, bump him under the chin with the top of his head, and wind in and out of his legs, tracing figures of eight, whilst he just stood there looking embarrassed. Red Dog still chased cats, but he made an exception for Red Cat. If anyone threatened his friend, it was Red Dog who ran up growling to defend him. He and Red Cat made quite a few dogs and foxes regret that they had ever ventured into their domain.

One evening Nancy took a picture of Red Dog fast asleep under the bougainvillea with Red Cat sleeping on top of him. She had two copies printed, sent one of them to a magazine, and had the other framed so that she could put it up on the wall.

RED DOG,
DON AND THE RANGER

Red Dog had travelled for about five years after John's death before he got to know the men at the Dampier Salt Company, and this only happened because of an accident.

He had hitched a lift with Peeto from Port Hedland back to Dampier, and had begun the journey safely enough, sitting in the front seat of the Ford Falcon, with his head out of the window as usual. The trouble was that he had eaten three sausages, a lamb chop, the remains of a steak and kidney pie, some baked beans and a bowl of cabbage with gravy at a hotel where he had befriended the cook. The consequence, of course, was another of his famous attacks of evil-smelling wind, and so Peeto had transferred him to the small trailer that he was towing behind his car.

This trailer was heaped with swags and other camping gear, because Peeto had been on a fishing trip in the crocodile-infested mangrove swamps of Broome, and so Red Dog had been obliged to sit on top of that swaying mound, trying not to get flung off every time that the vehicle braked or went around a corner. When they reached the junction where they were to turn off towards Dampier, however, Peeto tried to get out in a hurry so that he wouldn't have to wait for an approaching car. Red Dog was unprepared, as at that precise moment he was daydreaming about rabbits, and quite suddenly he went flying into the road, landing heavily and painfully, and twisting one of his hind legs. The car disappeared into the distance, the driver unaware that his famous passenger had parted company with him, and Red Dog hopped on three legs back to the side of the road.

Red Dog was quite used to falling off trailers, and out of the trays of utes, as these were common mishaps for Western Australian dogs, and he knew that he would feel better before long. If necessary, three legs would be quite sufficient for walking on for the time being.

It was a man called Don who spotted Red Dog limping towards Dampier. Don worked for Dampier Salt, the company that had transformed the landscape of the area by digging out huge, shallow rectangular pits that they filled with seawater. The water then dried away, leaving behind it the gleaming white carpets of salt that sparkled and shimmered in the bright sunshine.

If you stood on the high ground outside Dampier, you could look across the saltfields and see a great white mountain in the distance, where the company had heaped their harvest high, in preparation for processing.

Don knew all about Red Dog, and had often seen him round about, but they had never until now been introduced, which was why Red Dog didn't leap out in front of Don's car in order to try to stop it. Red Dog only stopped people he knew, or vehicles that he recognised.

Don stopped, however, and got out of his car. Red Dog lay down with his tongue hanging out, and allowed Don to roll him over. Don felt the injured leg gently, and said, 'Well, mate, I can't find anything wrong, but I reckon it's a trip to the vet for you.'

'Ah,' said the new vet, when Don brought the casualty in, 'it's Red Dog again.'

'You know him then,' said Don.

'I do now,' said the vet. 'For a long time I thought he was several dogs who all looked the same. Then I realised it was one dog with nine lives who belonged to everyone. Never heard of anything like it. Actually you can say I know him pretty well.'

'How's that, then?' asked Don.

''Cause he took a fancy to my little bitch, and he kept coming back, and then he decided he was going to camp out on my verandah. Well, that was all right with me, except that he started to think it was his place altogether, and that was when the trouble began. Whenever another male dog turned up, Red tried to see him

84

off, and then one day there was a dog that only came in for his jabs, and when he left he had five stitches.'

'Don't suppose Red liked it when another dog came near his sheila,' laughed Don.

'Exactly,' agreed the vet, nodding his head. 'So anyway, I had to tell him to leave, 'cause I can't have him assaulting my customers. So off he went, and now he just comes back to say hello. He gets some tucker and a snooze on the porch, and then he's off. You know what he does? He recognises any car from Dampier, and he goes and sits next to it 'til the driver comes back.' The vet ruffled Red Dog's ears, and added, 'No hard feelings, eh mate?'

The vet examined Red Dog's leg but couldn't find any breaks or fractures, so he decided that it was probably badly bruised. 'I just want to see something,' he said to Don, and he went to his cupboard and took out a new syringe, which he removed carefully from its sterilised plastic wrapping.

'What are you gonna do, doc?' asked Don. 'Give him an anaesthetic?'

'No,' replied the vet, 'it's just that I've noticed that Red isn't quite his old self any more.'

'Well, he's getting on a bit, isn't he? Grey hairs on his snout. Does anyone know how old he is?'

'About eight, I think.'

'Well, what do you think might be wrong?'

The vet looked thoughtful, and said, 'He's eight, and he's spent his life travelling, and roughing it when he has to, so he's got a right to be tired. But he's a tough fella, and just recently he's been losing fights and getting hurt more than he ought to. I'm going to check him out for heartworm.'

'Oh, yuk,' said Don, 'what's that?'

'Just what it sounds like,' said the vet. 'It's a worm that circulates in the blood when it's a larva, and lives in the heart when it grows up. Sometimes you get a great fistful of them living in there, and then the dog can die. It's getting more common, and I've got a feeling that's what's up with Red. The trouble is, I'm going to have to keep him for quite a while, and this clinic isn't even finished. I haven't had the cages put in yet. Can you keep him under lock and key until I get the results?'

'No worries,' said Don.

Later on the vet made a slide of a tiny sample of Red Dog's blood, and placed it under the microscope. He was having a campaign against heartworm, and he found the whole business of detecting it and then getting rid of it to be quite exciting. It was a well-known problem further north, but in this region he was something of a pioneer, and it was proving to be more widespread than anyone had suspected. He adjusted the focus with the knurled wheel, and there, sure enough, were dozens of the heartworm microfilaria swimming about in Red Dog's blood. 'Gotcha,' he said.

The vet did not particularly want to have Red Dog living with him whilst he underwent treatment, because it was bad idea to have him biting his other customers.

He also realised that Don would be unable to keep Red Dog confined, because he would escape at the first opportunity, and that would spoil the effectiveness of the treatment. Then he had a brainwave, and he rang the ranger.

The ranger was responsible for rounding up stray dogs and keeping them in a pen until their owners came to collect them.

'Right, mate,' said the ranger, when the vet had told him what he wanted, 'but, you see, Red Dog isn't really a stray, is he? He's a sort of professional traveller.'

'But he doesn't belong to anyone, so he must be a stray.'

'I see your point, but I can only hold dogs in the pound until the owner comes for them, and then they have to pay for the upkeep. So who's going to pay for Red Dog?'

The vet was slightly shocked; 'Red Dog doesn't have to pay! Red Dog's in common.'

There was a pause at the other end of the line, and then the ranger sighed. 'Well, I dare say,' he said, 'I can keep him in the pound while you do the treatment. I can't say I'm happy about it, 'cause the budget's tight enough as it is, but since it's Red Dog we're talking about . . .'

So it was that Red Dog was confined to the dog-pound with the stray dogs of Roebourne Shire, and funnily enough, he seemed quite happy about it. He appeared to know that whereas the other dogs were humble captives, he was an honoured guest, and so he shamelessly lorded it over the other dogs, keeping them in their place and being firm with them if ever they got out of line. For the time being he gave up his yearning for constant travel, and relaxed as if he were on holiday. He was so good that he even went out with the ranger to look for strays, sitting up in the front seat of the ranger's yellow ute, whilst the strays were tied up in the back. In the meantime he submitted to all the tests and injections as if he were good-naturedly humouring the vet.

Back at the single men's quarters of Dampier Salt, Don told the others about how Red Dog was confined to the pound whilst he was being treated. Someone from Dampier Salt told someone else that Red Dog was in the pound, and then someone told Vanno at Hamersley Iron.

Peeto, Vanno and Jocko were horrified. 'Jeez,' said Peeto, 'ain't that where they kill the strays?'

'Only if they can't find the owner,' said Jocko.

'Red Dog, he ain't got an owner,' said Peeto. 'Only Red Dog owns Red Dog.'

'They wouldn't put down Red Dog,' said Vanno.

'The world's full of people who'd put down Red Dog,' said Peeto. 'The world's a bad place, and it's only getting badder.'

The men thought about it for a while, and before long their anger and concern got the better of them. 'There's only one thing to do,' said Jocko at last.

That night, at two in the morning, the three men drove to Roebourne. Outside the ranger's pound they put on gloves, and Vanno took a large pair of boltcutters from the boot of the car. They were three foot long, capable of cutting through thick iron rods, and they seemed to weigh a ton.

They felt just like commandos as they crept towards the wire. An owl shrieked in a Christmas tree, and they nearly jumped out of their skins. Peeto tripped over Vanno and they all said 'shhhhhh' to each other. The dogs began to bark, and Peeto said, 'We gotta be quick.'

Vanno cut the hasp of the lock with his boltcutters,

and slipped inside. Hastily he pulled a torch from his pocket, and flashed its light from one dog to another. They were barking like crazy, making a terrible noise and fuss, and he began to regret coming on this expedition at all. It occurred to him that not only might he get caught, but any one of these mutts might give him a good biting. 'Red,' he whispered, 'Red, where are you?'

He felt a muzzle nudging at his hand, and he snatched it away because he thought he was about to be attacked. He looked down, and there was the unmistakably robust shadow of Red Dog. He thrust the torch back into his pocket, picked the dog up, tucked him under his arm, and ran out, making sure that none of the other captives escaped with him.

His co-conspirators patted him on the back and whispered their congratulations. They piled back into the car and sped away, whooping with relief and happiness, and Red Dog licked their faces and nipped at their hands. Back in Dampier they went to Peeto's hut and drank a few stubbies to celebrate, repeating the highlights of their exploit.

'Jeez,' said Peeto, 'that owl near killed me with fright. I almost had a little accident.'

'I thought we were done for,' said Jocko, 'when the dogs set to barking.'

'Hey,' said Vanno, patting Red Dog on the head, and cupping his chin in his hand, 'just look what your mates are prepared to do for you,'

The next morning the ranger glumly rang up the vet and told him that Red Dog had been kidnapped during the night.

'Oh no,' said the vet, 'it's a disaster. I've only done half the treatment.'

'We'll have to find him and bring him back,' said the ranger.

'Yes, but how? You know what he's like. He could easily be in Carnarvon by now, or down at Tom Price.'

'We'll just have to ask around,' said the ranger, 'and follow up any leads.'

'Why would anyone kidnap him?' demanded the vet, exasperated. 'It's so damned stupid.'

'Probably thought we were going to put him down,' said the ranger. 'That fella's got lots of friends.'

The two men resigned themselves to having lost their patient, and to leaving him full of the lethal worms until he showed up again, and the ranger hung up. He got his keys from the kitchen, finished his cup of coffee and went outside into the blazing light. In the distance there was a beautiful mirage of a sailing ship in full sail above the horizon, and the ranger stopped for a moment to marvel at it. Then he got into his vehicle and drove off in the direction of the Miaree Pool. He stopped for petrol and went inside to pay the cashier.

When he came out, he stuffed his wallet back into his pocket and then walked towards his yellow ute. The ranger could hardly believe his eyes, because there was Red Dog sitting next to the passenger door, asking to be let it. The ranger put his hand to his forehead, shook his head, and laughed.

So it was that Red Dog finished his treament for heartworm and took on a new lease of life. He went to find Don at the Dampier Salt Company, and made friends with the men there. They were the same kind as those who worked at Hamersley Iron: exiles, foreigners, transients, people earning a fast buck so that they could start a new life elsewhere. They seldom stayed for long, but always the tradition and custom of caring for Red Dog survived.

He was allowed to stay in whichever hut he liked; all he had to do was scratch at the door and he was welcomed in. The blokes made him a member of the union and the sports and social club, they kept a timesheet and they gave him a book of canteen tickets. His job was to polish off the leftovers. Don opened a bank account for him with the Wales Bank, under the name 'Red Dog', and money was paid into it whenever the lads had a whip-round to raise funds for his vet's bills. Don also registered him with the shire, so that he would no longer run the risk of being classified as a stray, and his official title became 'The Dog of the North-West.'

That may have been his official title, but at Dampier Salt he acquired another name altogether. In Australia anyone with red hair shares the common fate of being called 'Bluey', and that's what they called him, too.

RED DOG
AND THE DREADED CRIBBAGES

Back in the time when there were almost no houses
and only two caravan parks in Karratha, Red Dog liked
to call in on the caravans that belonged to his many
friends and providers. He would expect to be washed,
de-ticked, and fed, and then he would stay a couple of
days until he felt like setting off on his travels once more.

Red Dog particularly liked one of the parks, because
that was where his mate Red Cat lived, as well as Nancy
and Patsy, but, and it was a big BUT, there was one small
problem. Actually, the truth is that there were two big
problems, and they were married to each other.

Mr and Mrs Cribbage were the caretakers of the
caravan park. They lived off pigsnout sandwiches,
sweet milky tea, and cigarettes, and it was their duty to
keep the place tidy and neat. They would sort out any

difficulties that people might have with water-supply or electricity. If the bulbs blew in the dunnies, Mr Cribbage would sigh with irritation and change them. If Red Cat raided a bin and overturned it, it was Mrs Cribbage who would sigh with irritation and set it upright. This is all to say that they were fairly typical caretakers, who were seldom pleased when their leisure was interrupted by their jobs, or when their cups of tea had to be abandoned in mid-sip.

The unfortunate thing about Mr and Mrs Cribbage was that they were pernickety about enforcing the rules, even the stupid ones that any normal person would ignore, and one of these rules was 'NO DOGS'.

The first time that Mrs Cribbage met Red Dog, he was just about to scratch on the door of Patsy's caravan. 'Hey, you!' she called, rushing up to him and waving a dishcloth in his face. 'Be off with you! Shoo! Shoo!'

Red Dog looked at this fat woman and her dish-cloth, and decided that she was probably mad. He ignored her politely, and scratched once more on Patsy's door.

'Off! Away!' shouted Mrs Cribbage, and at that moment Patsy opened her door. She looked from the dog to the woman, and asked, 'What's up?'

'NO DOGS!' announced Mrs Cribbage.

Patsy regarded her pityingly and told her, 'This isn't any old dog. This is Red Dog.'

'A dog's a dog,' replied Mrs Cribbage, 'and I don't care if it's one of the Queen's bloody corgis. This is a dog, and that's that. NO DOGS.' It occurred to Patsy that Mrs.Cribbage's voice sounded rather like a kookaburra.

'Red Dog has privileges,' said Patsy. 'Everyone knows that.'

'If you don't get rid of that dog,' said Mrs Cribbage, her voice rising still further, 'you'll have me and Mr Cribbage to answer to.'

'If you try to get rid of Red Dog, you'll have the whole of the Pilbara to answer to,' replied Nancy, 'so if I were you I wouldn't get my knickers in a knot.'

Mrs Cribbage huffed, 'And if you don't get rid of that dog, we'll shoot it, and evict you too. So don't say you didn't get warned.'

Mrs Cribbage turned her back and walked away importantly, confident that she, and only she, was queen in this little kingdom. Over the next few days, however, she kept thinking that she saw Red Dog out of the corner of her eye, and she mentioned it several times to Mr Cribbage, who was a small man with a toothbrush moustache rather like Hitler's. His moustache and his fingers were a nasty shade of yellowy-brown, rather like a pub ceiling, because he liked to smoke all the time, rolling himself tiny, tight little cigarettes. When he finished smoking one, he would open the butt-end and take out the unsmoked tobacco so that he could use it again in another cigarette. He had become hollow-chested, and you always knew when he was coming, because of his perpetual dry cough.

The couple went into Dampier and bought a stencil

from the stationer's in the mall, and then they spent a happy morning making lots of notices and signboards that said 'NO DOGS'. These they stuck up on every available tree in the caravan park, after which they felt that they had done a good day's work indeed. The people in the park shook their heads, and agreed that from now on they would have a coded alarm, so that the caretakers would never catch them out when Red Dog was about. Patsy proposed that their code-word should be 'pussycats', and this was soon adopted. Mr and Mrs Cribbage wondered for quite a while why it was that people shouted 'pussycats', without provocation, every time that they passed by with their buckets and bins. 'I reckon they're all barking mad,' observed Mr Cribbage.

'Talking of barking, I still keep seeing that dog,' said his wife.

Now, it so happened that both Patsy and Nancy were scared of the dark. Back then there were almost no lights to make the sky glow orange, and you could see every star in the sky as brightly as if it were sparkling on the tips of your fingers. The moon lay on its back as if on holiday, setting down its cool watery light. If it was cloudy, however, you would not be able to see anything at all if your torch batteries ran out, and many poor souls found themselves shivering until dawn, absolutely lost even though they were only a few steps from their door.

Red Dog could smell his way around in the dark,

96

as if his nose were an extra pair of eyes, but he did seem to understand that Patsy and Nancy were scared. Accordingly, when they needed to go to the dunny at night, he would turn up at their sides as if by magic, and then escort them back to their caravans again. They were grateful for this help, and rewarded him with plenty of snacks and affection. Before Red Dog's arrival, Red Cat had been the official protector of the site, but he had never provided as good a free service as this.

As mischance would have it, one night Mrs Cribbage needed to go at the same time as Patsy, and she caught her with Red Dog, strolling out of the dunny in the moonlight. She stopped in her tracks for a moment, puffed out her cheeks and worked up a good head of anger, until she had succeeded in making herself as mad as a cut snake. 'What's this?' she cried, 'What's this? You've still got that dog. What did I tell you? It's eviction for you, my girl, that's what.'

Patsy knew that if she was evicted she would have nowhere else to go, but at this moment she didn't seem to care. She had had enough of the Cribbages and their anti-dog campaign. She was cold, and she just wanted to get back to bed. Suddenly she heard herself saying, 'Aw, get lost, why don't you?'

'Cow!' exclaimed Mrs Cribbage. 'Bitch! Just you wait!'

'I'll wait,' said Nancy. She looked down at Red Dog, whose yellow eyes were glowing in the moonlight.

'Come on Red, let's go back to bed.' Without another word she turned her back on Mrs Cribbage and coolly walked away.

The next morning, whilst she was having breakfast, she heard a rustling noise, and saw that a note was being pushed under her door. It was written in tiny neat handwriting:

Due to you're being persistantly and unreasonnably in vyolation of the rules with respeck to dogs, you are hearby noterfied that as from tomorrow morning you are deklared evickted from this park and tomorrow morning at 9.30 I shall be ariving with a vehcle to tow you out of it. Sincerely, Mr and Mrs Cribbage.

Patsy read this note twice, and then took it round to Nancy's, saying, 'What am I going to do? Where am I going to live? This is just awful! They're going to make me homeless, just because of a dog!'

98

Nancy twisted her lip and shook her head. 'What a pair of dingbats. And just look at that spelling!' She put her hand on Patsy's arm. 'Don't you worry,' she said, 'and don't start packing either, 'cause I'm going to make sure that you don't have to go anywhere at all.' She took the note and went from caravan to caravan, in order to show it to everyone she could find.

The following morning at 9.20, Mr Cribbage straightened his greasy old tie, combed his Hitler moustache and arranged the few strands of his hair across his bald patch.

'There's an awful lot of people driving around this morning,' observed Mrs Cribbage, who was standing at the window. 'I wonder what they can all be up to.'

Mr Cribbage picked up his keys from the table, squared his shoulders, coughed and opened the door. He was feeling satisfied and fulfilled, because he was just about to exercise his power and authority. 'Now they'll take me seriously,' he was thinking.

99

Once he was outside, however, his pleasure quickly turned to gall.

For a moment he could hardly believe what he saw. Some of the inhabitants of the park had left their cars all around his, so that he was completely boxed in, and others had abandoned their vehicles all over the tracks that wound between the caravans. Worse than this, perhaps, the people themselves were standing around in small groups, smiling at him and gloating over his discomfiture.

'Reckon on towing Patsy out, do you?' called one, and nudged the person next to him.

'Want any help?' called another.

'Reckon you might have a problem,' called yet another.

Mr Cribbage felt fury and frustration rise up in his breast. His lips quivered, his eyes popped, sweat broke out on his forehead and his heart thumped. He spoke at last. 'Have it your way, then. That dog's a stray, and I'm calling in the ranger. It'll be put down, and that'll be the end of it.'

'That's no bloody use,' called someone. 'Red's the ranger's mate. And he ain't a stray either. He's registered.'

The caretaker stood for a moment quite still, and then turned on his heel and marched back into his office.

People were just wondering what was happening, when he re-emerged. In his hands was a twelve-bore shotgun. He broke the barrel, took two cartridges out of his coat pocket and slipped them into the chambers. He snapped the barrel shut and looked up at the caravaners, who by now were feeling distinctly uneasy. He put the gun under his left arm and patted it with his right hand. 'When I see that dog,' he announced, 'he's getting both barrels of this.' He turned round and went back inside. He took the cartridges out of the gun and propped it up in a corner. He was trembling with anger and with spite as he said to Mrs Cribbage, 'I'm going to have to shoot that dog.'

'You should shoot some of those drongos whilst you're about it,' said Mrs Cribbage, huffing. 'They're scum, nothing but scum. Got no respect, no respect at all, they haven't.'

Outside, things began to move quickly. 'I can't believe it,' people said to each other, 'the bastard actually wants to shoot Red Dog.'

'It can't be legal,' said others. 'He can't do that.'

'I'm calling the RSPCA,' announced Patsy.

'I'm calling the boys at Hamersley Iron,' said Nancy.

That afternoon the RSPCA officer arrived, and in no uncertain terms threatened the Cribbages with prosecution. But that was not the worst of it. Later still, a yellow bus arrived from Hamersley Iron. The workers inside had only just finished their shifts, and fatigue had made them feel doubly upset. Some of them were covered in soot, or with red dust, or with machine oil. They were fierce, hard men, and they were very angry indeed. They burst into Mr Cribbage's office without

101

knocking, and the caretakers' cups of tea stopped mid-way to their lips. They were completely surrounded. Jocko put his hands on the desk and leaned forward; 'Now would you be the wee little scumbag that we've been hearing about?'

The next morning, very early, Patsy knocked on Nancy's door and told her, 'You won't believe this, Nance, but the Cribbages have gone.'

It was true. They had left their jobs without notice, and without collecting their pay. Their allotment was now a bare rectangle of brown concrete in the middle of a scruffy lawn and a couple of badly tended flower-beds. It looked most strange.

'I feel terrible,' said Patsy, later. 'We've gone and run them out of town. It's not exactly what you might call civilised, is it?'

'It's too late to regret it now,' said Nancy, 'They've gone. No-one's going to miss them either.'

'All the same,' replied Patsy, 'I don't feel too good about it.'

It was true; their victory had a bitter taste, and even Red Dog did not seem to derive much pleasure from it. He went looking for John one more time, hitched a lift to sweet Adelaide on a semi-trailer and came back two months later on a road-train. By the time he next scratched on Nancy's door there were new caretakers and new rules.

THE LAST JOURNEY

For all of us there comes a time when the luck runs out. Fate stops smiling, and we have to face our last struggle. Some of us are physically alone when we die, and some not, but whether or no, it is not possible to travel in company through that last dark tunnel at the end of life.

Red Dog was only eight years old, but he had had a tough existence, riding all over Western Australia looking for his lost master, getting in fights, eating too much some of the time, too little at other times, getting shot at, falling off the backs of utes and lorries, freezing at night and roasting by day. His dark-red muzzle became flecked with grey, his limbs stiffened and sometimes he felt just a little too tired to chase the shadows of birds on the oval. When he travelled in search of John he sometimes had to be helped into the vans, cars and trains that he wanted to board. Worst of all, though, was the casual malice of some of the human beings who crossed his path. Nobody knows why it is that some people derive satisfaction from acts of cruelty; all we know is that such people exist, and that quite often their chosen victims are animals.

One day Nancy was grooming him, when she found bullet holes through his ears. That was one more of his narrow escapes, but then one Saturday in November Peeto was driving in his ute from Karratha to Dampier, when out of the corner of his eye he thought he saw something dark red in the stones at the side of the road. Whatever it was, it was lying on the ground, and it was quivering.

He backed up and got out. He looked down in horror for just a moment, and then realised that he would have to do something. The trouble was that Red Dog was writhing and twisting so much that Peeto couldn't keep a hold on him. It was as if Red had gone mad, or was completely out of control. In his amber eyes was an expression of terrible pain and desperation. 'Oh jeez; oh jeez,' Peeto muttered to himself as he struggled to keep the dog still and lift him into his ute. It was hopeless. Red Dog was heavy, solid and still very strong.

Fortunately for Peeto, Bill the policeman drove by shortly afterwards, and he spotted Peeto's car at the side of the road, with Peeto apparently struggling with something next to it. Bill and Peeto had never really got along since Bill had charged Peeto with drunk-driving whilst coming home with Red Dog from Port Hedland all those years before, after Red Dog had been shot. They were near neighbours, it is true, but it is hard for policemen to enjoy a normal social life when sometimes they have to impose the law on their own friends.

Bill thought that he had better stop, however, in case Peeto was in some kind of trouble. This is the code all over rural Australia, and everyone observes it. In this case it was only a moment before he and Peeto had forgotten their differences altogether.

The two men battled to get Red Dog into the back of the ute. It was frightening to have to try to control an animal, who was also an old and well-loved friend, who was thrashing about in their arms as if possessed by a devil. Peeto and Bill swore and winced as Red Dog's claws raked across their faces, and swore all over again when Red began to vomit.

Finally they heaved Red Dog into the vehicle, and stood back for a breather. 'What the hell is it?' asked Peeto, gesturing towards the suffering animal.

'It's poison, mate,' said Bill. 'Strychnine. I've seen it before. They get these convulsions that last for hours, and then they die.'

'Who'd give Red poison, for God's sake? He's every-one's pet dog.'

Bill pursed his lips and shook his head knowingly. 'The things I've seen since I was a policeman, you just wouldn't believe. I'll tell you, mate, there's no animal lower than us in the whole damn world.' He looked at Peeto and said, 'We'd better get him to the vet, mate.'

They looked at Red in his agony, and Peeto said, 'Let's take him to the copshop, and call the vet out. I don't reckon it'll do him any good to have to go all the way to Roebourne.'

So it was that Red Dog was driven to the police station and laid down on the table, where Bill tried to hold him still whilst Peeto called the vet. He spoke urgently into the phone, and then came back looking grim.

'The vet's away,' he said. 'I've left a message, but they don't know when he'll be back.'

Peeto took over from Bill in the battle to hold Red Dog still. He grasped Red Dog by the upper forearms, and then looked sideways at the policeman. He said, 'There's only one thing we can do. We can't let it go on. I can't bloody bear it.'

'You're right,' said Bill, 'but I don't want to.'

'You've got to, mate,' said Peeto softly. 'If he carries on like this he's going to break his own bones. You can't look at him like this and think there's any hope.'

'I've got to account for every bullet,' said Bill. 'I don't know if I'm supposed to be putting down dogs.'

'Listen, we'll all back you up. No-one's going to give you a bashing for helping out a poor old dog.'

'Yeah, well, I guess you're right,' said Bill. 'I guess you're right. But even so . . .'

'You've got to, mate. Red would thank you for it.'

'We'll take him outside,' said Bill. 'We can't do it indoors. I know that much.'

Between them they picked up the convulsing dog, and carried him out into the sunshine. They laid him on the red earth. A squad of tiny pigeons called to each other in a nearby palm tree, seeming to mock each other. Bill unbuckled the flap on his holster. He took out his pistol, loaded the chamber with two bullets and stood silently for a moment. Peeto saw that his eyes were filling with tears.

He knelt down and stroked Red Dog's head with the back of his hand. 'I'm sorry, mate,' he said, 'I don't want to do this, and you've got to forgive me.'

Red Dog was too raddled with the poison to know what was happening, let alone to understand or forgive. It was as if the poison had removed his personality and his identity. He was nothing but a living heap of contorting pain.

Bill knelt down and put the muzzle to Red's fore-head, between the eyes, but could not hold the gun steady because the dog was convulsing too much. 'We've got to hold him still,' said Bill. 'Otherwise I can't do it.'

'I can't hold his head,' said Peeto, desperately. 'He's moving around so much, I might get shot in the hand.'

Just then, Red Dog fell still for a moment, and Bill put the gun to his head once more. He took up first pressure on the trigger, and closed his eyes. Peeto bit his lip, looked away and awaited the report of the pistol. Then Bill sat back suddenly on his heels. 'I'm sorry,' he said, 'I can't do it. I just can't do it.'

Thus it was that Peeto called up Red Dog's friends, and they arrived one by one to take it in turns to hold onto him and quell the convulsions during the long hours until the vet's arrival. No-one held out any hope for Red Dog's survival, and as they drank tea in the crowded little police station they reminisced about their old friend whom they were about to lose.

'I remember once,' said Nancy, 'I went to the Miaree Pool with my family, and we had the cat in the back, for some reason, and anyway, when we arrived, there was Red fast asleep on a mudbank. The trees were full of white cockatoos, and the water was just right for bathing. It was really lovely. We spent the day lying around in our bathers, swimming, picnicking, all the usual, and then when it was late we got ready to go home. That was when Red decided he wanted a lift, and he tried to jump in the back. We shoved him out again, 'cause we thought it wasn't fair on the cat. You know Red liked to chase cats, apart from Red Cat at the caravan park. It was difficult, 'cause we knew Red would need a lift, and we felt bad about shoving him out.

'Anyway, you know that track to the pool is pretty rough, so we drove away slowly, like you do, and then after a while we realised that Red was trotting along beside the car, still asking for a lift, so we told him to go away, but he still wouldn't give up.

'Finally we stopped the car, and we said, "OK, Red, we give in, but you're not coming in here unless you leave the cat alone." So Red jumped in, and he sat there as good as gold, with his head out of the window, all the way back to Dampier, without giving the cat any gyp at all. And the funny thing is, the cat wasn't bothered a bit.'

'He was obstinate all right,' said Patsy. 'I remember one time Red missed the bus into Dampier, so he ran out in front of the car and stopped me instead. I thought I'd take him back to my place, but when we got there, he wouldn't get out. Just sat there looking at me sideways, with the whites of his eyes showing. So I got back in and chased after that bus, and I caught it near the terminal. I told Red to get out, but he wouldn't. I suppose he wanted me to take him all the way to the mess. Anyway, I went up to the bus and knocked on the window, and I said to that driver, "Do me a favour, I've chased you all the way from Karratha, and I've got a meal to cook. Can you get that dog out of my car?"'

'The driver put his hand in his mouth and whistled, and Red jumped out, good as gold, and went and sat behind him in the bus, and that was the last I saw of him until nine o'clock that night, when there's a scratching at the door. You guessed; after all that trouble, he only decided to come and stay with me after all.'

'I picked him up once,' said Ellen. 'It was two in the morning, 'cause I was picking my girl up from the disco. He wouldn't get out at Poon's Camp, and then he wouldn't get out at Dampier mess, and we were getting pretty tired and fed up, I can tell you. Finally we took him to Hamersley Iron single-quarters, and he hopped out. As he jumped out, he did a really filthy smell, like it was some kind of a thank-you!'

'His guts were always a liability,' said Peeto. 'You know, once when he tried to pull that cadging-lifts trick on me, we put him in the boss's ute and just left him there. The boss still don't know who did it. He wasn't too pleased with that stink when he opened the door.'

'I remember,' said Bill, 'when he used to come in the patrol car when we were testing it out for speed after a service. He didn't care how fast I went. He just stuck his head out of the window as normal, with the wind whistling through his ears.'

'Yeah, but he wasn't stupid,' said Vanno. 'One day I see this drunk driving along, weaving all over the road, with Red in the passenger seat, and the drunk stops for a leak, you know, he does it in public 'cause he's so far gone he doesn't care, and Red just jumps out of the window and trots into the bush. Then he comes out and begs another lift from the car coming after. That's one bright dog.'

'Everyone's got a Red Dog story,' said Jocko. 'Some-one ought to write them down.'

They all sat in silence for a while, taking it in turns to control Red Dog's lashing and shaking. By the time the vet arrived the following morning, they were all hollow-eyed with exhaustion and pity.

The vet listened to Red's heart through a stethoscope and shook his head. 'It's strychnine,' he said, confirming Bill's diagnosis. 'I guess he must have eaten dingo bait.'

'There aren't any dingoes here,' said Peeto. 'Leastways, I've never seen one.'

'People leave out poison anyway,' said the vet, sighing. 'The stationmen blame wild dogs and dingoes for just about everything, and nowadays you've even got people who put out poison for cats, 'cause they're not a native species. It makes me sick. It's me who has to cope with the consequences.'

'Yeah, well,' reflected Peeto, 'None of us is a native species either.'

The vet looked sadly down at his old mate on the table, and Patsy asked, 'Are you going to put him down?'

'I damn well ought to,' said the vet. 'He's a strong old dog, though, and I'm going to give him a chance. You know something? I'm going to miss him if he dies. I went right out into the middle of nowhere once, to deal with a sick old brumby, and when I got there, there was Red sitting next to it on the straw. He always knew where the action was.' He paused and then said, 'I'm going to have to ask four of you to hold him still while I give him an injection. He mustn't move at all. I can't have the needle breaking off. Understood?'

It was almost impossible to keep the animal immobile, but finally the vet jabbed the needle into him and quickly pressed down on the plunger. Red Dog's friends watched with bated breath as his twitching and shaking gradually subsided, until finally he lay still. 'Hey, doc,' said Vanno, in a hushed and admiring voice. 'It's a bloody miracle.'

'It's an anti-convulsant,' said the vet. 'I ought to have made him sick first, to get the rest of the poison out, but I think it would have killed him.' He looked round at Red Dog's friends and said, 'You guys look pretty tired. You must have put in some damn hard yakka. You may as well take time out. I'm going to keep him under until the convulsions wear off, and it could be a couple of days.'

The vet kept Red Dog unconscious for two and half days, administering small doses of anti-convulsant every time that the shaking and writhing began to start up again, and after that it took Red another twelve hours to get to his feet. In the meantime a rumour had gone round the shire that Red Dog was dead, and the local paper printed a story reporting the poisoning, but saying that Red had made a recovery.

Certainly, that was how it seemed. He was clumsy and unsteady, but he emptied his bowl of food, wagged his tail when his well-wishers called in, and even escaped for a while to the Walkabout Hotel, where he knew there were people who were generous with tasty titbits. The effort of going there was too much for him, however, and the vet came round to fetch him back.

Everyone was elated at Red Dog's recovery, and he began to receive cards at the vet's surgery, but the vet had a bad feeling about it all, and was not altogether surprised when Red Dog's clumsiness began to get worse. He was walking into the furniture, falling over sideways and then struggling valiantly but hopelessly to get up. He still had his appetite, but finally that was all that he did have left. The vet rang around his friends.

'He's been falling over, and now he can't get up at all. It's obvious that he's got brain damage. He's not himself, and he's never going to be. You know, you can look in an animal's eyes, and when the light goes out, you know it's time to give in. I'm really sorry. We tried, but now we've got to finish. Anything else would be too unkind.'

Patsy, Ellen, Nancy, Bill, the ranger and some of the boys from Dampier Salt and Hamersley Iron all called in to say goodbye to Red Dog. The men tried not to show their feelings, because that's how Aussie men are, but their throats were so choked with sorrow that none of them could speak. They patted Red where he lay, unable to get up, and ruffled his ears for the last time. Silently they filed out, unwilling to look each other in the eye in case they lost control. Only Vanno cried, because he was Italian, and that was all right in Italy, so no-one could lay any blame. Between his tears Vanno swore that if he ever found out who it was that had poisoned Red Dog, there was going to be hell to pay, and that's for sure.

The women came in and kissed Red Dog on the top of his head, stroking his neck and weeping. One by one they knelt down and hugged him, feeling as sad and desolate as if they had lost a child. When they had left, the vet came in with a syringe full of morphine, and shaved a small patch on Red's right foreleg. He made his own private farewells to this character who had been so much a part of his life since he had arrived in this hard and captivating part of Australia. He thought about how much the place had changed in the few years of Red Dog's life. Now there were houses instead of caravans, and tarmac in the place of stones. It was as if the passing of Red Dog symbolised the passing of old Roebourne Shire.

He thought about how he used to think that Red was lots of different dogs that all looked the same, about how many times he had dealt with Red Dog's accidents and emergencies, and how few times he had ever actually been paid for it. He thought about how much he would miss this obstinate, valiant soul, who seemed such a typical Western Australian, even though he was only a dog. He looked into Red's sad, tired and pained eyes, stroked his head and said, 'Time to go, old mate, time to go.' He breathed deeply a couple of times in order to overcome his regret and steady his mind, and then he performed the lethal injection. He watched as Red Dog's eyes glazed over. Then he lowered Red's body gently as he slumped sideways on the table and drifted off to his last long sleep.

Who knows what went through Red Dog's dreams as he lay dying? Perhaps he was young again, galloping back from the airfield in Paraburdoo. Perhaps he was chasing the shadows of birds on the oval, or out in the

114

bush chasing wallabies, or in the caravan park, watching the scarlet sunset with Red Cat. After half a lifetime of looking for John, perhaps in that final dream he found him.

Bill and the vet buried Red Dog in a simple grave in the bush between Roebourne and Cossack. They laid him in that stony red earth and covered him over. It was a hot day, a day when Red might otherwise have been lounging in the air-conditioned mall at Dampier, or taking the ore train to Mt Tom Price. There is no-one now who remembers where that grave was, and no headstone was ever placed above it. His friends eventually raised a bronze monument to him in Dampier, but otherwise there is nothing left of Red Dog but the stories, and his collar, whose tag reads 'Red Dog – Bluey' on one side, and 'I've been everywhere, mate' on the other.

GLOSSARY OF AUSTRALIANISMS

Akubra: kind of brimmed hat popular in Australia.

Barbie: barbecue.

Bathers: swimsuit.

Bilby: small marsupial, somewhat similar to a rabbit.

Blotto on Rotto: getting drunk on Rottnest Island, a holiday island and nature reserve off Fremantle, famous for its colony of quokkas.

Bludging: scrounging.

Blue: a violent dispute.

Bombs: farts.

Brumby: wild horse.

Bundy: Bundaberg rum, a popular Australian rum. Every Aussie gets horribly drunk on it at least once in a lifetime.

Crinkled cassia: plant common in the Pilbara.

Dag: someone revolting.

Daggy: revolting.

Damper: crude bread made without yeast, much relied on by the early pioneers.

Dingbat: fool.

Dingo: Australian wild dog that is supposed to have arrived with the aborigines.

Drongo: slow-witted person.

Dunny: lavatory.

Emu: very large flightless bird. Also a popular brand of beer.

Esky: insulated plastic hamper for keeping food and drink cool when you are travelling.

Freo: Fremantle, a pretty town on the Swan River that serves as the port to Perth.

Going bush: disappearing on your own.

Gum trees: eucalyptus trees. Australia has an amazing number of different kinds.

Holden: Australian car manufacturer.

Kelpie: Australian breed of sheepdog.

Kookaburra: large bird of the kingfisher family, with a loud call that is often thought to resemble raucous laughter.

Mall: enclosed shopping centre.

Middy: beer.

Pigsnout sandwich: enormous sandwich suitable for a really greedy person.

Pilbara: mining region in Western Australia.

Quokka: marsupial that looks rather like a very big rat. There is a large colony of them on Rottnest Island.

Quoll: small marsupial, somewhat like a mouse.

Road-train: enormous lorry that tows two or more large trailers behind it.

Roo-trail: track left in vegetation when used regularly by kangaroos.

Servo: garage, petrol or service station.

Sheila: woman or girlfriend.

Shout: turn to buy the drinks.

Smoko: tea-break.

Snaggers: sausages.

Spinifex: prickly undergrowth.

Stairway to the moon: when the moon is very low on the sea at Pretty Pool, near Port Hedland, the glow of moonlight on the wavelets looks like a staircase with the moon at the top of it.

Stubbie: can of beer.

Swag: kind of bedroll used by Australians for sleeping rough.

Tops: excellent.

Trusty: an Aussie dogfood.

Tucker: food.

Ute: pick-up truck.

Walkabout: a wander in the wilderness. Originally part of the initiation of young aborigines.

Wallaroos: medium-sized animals very similar to wallabies and kangaroos.

Yakka: work.